# BULLS AMONGST MEN

C.S. QUINN

# COPYRIGHT © 2025
# CONNOR J. SUBOCZ-QUINN

# CONTENTS

Introduction                                                  v

PART ONE
**FREE-RANGE**
Chapter 1                                                      3
Chapter 2                                                      9
Chapter 3                                                      16
Chapter 4                                                      20
Chapter 5                                                      26
Chapter 6                                                      29

PART TWO
**THE RUN**
Chapter 7                                                      35
Chapter 8                                                      37
Chapter 9                                                      40
Chapter 10                                                     44
Chapter 11                                                     48
Chapter 12                                                     50
Chapter 13                                                     55

PART THREE
**TERCIO DE VARAS**
Chapter 14                                                     63
Chapter 15                                                     67
Chapter 16                                                     73
Chapter 17                                                     76
Chapter 18                                                     80
Chapter 19                                                     86

PART FOUR
**TERCIO DE BANDERILLAS**
Chapter 20                                                     101
Chapter 21                                                     106

Chapter 22     111
Chapter 23     115
Chapter 24     118
Chapter 25     134

PART FIVE
**TERCIO DE MUERTE**
Chapter 26     141
Chapter 27     152
Chapter 28     156
Chapter 29     160
Chapter 30     168
Chapter 31     174
Chapter 32     179
Chapter 33     184
Chapter 34     190

PART SIX
**POBRE DE MI**
Chapter 35     197

Authors Notes and Acknowledgments     201

# INTRODUCTION

**Andalucía, Spain 1885**

The storm has come and scattered them. Scattered with the lightening and the thunder and the rain. Murciélago and the others would be ready to fight, ready to run. The call to run wild is always with them. Domestication would be a crueler fate than death for their kind. He'd have to take caution today. They were just like a part of him. That recognition of them within him helped keep him grounded. Even when it stormed.

The sun was quarter of the way to noon and doing its best to dry the Andalusian hills. The spring weather still held a chill, so he threw on his short coat over his shirt, put on his flat cap over his head. Passed his wife and children, busy cleaning up after breakfast, and went out to the barn. As he walked, he tilted his chin up to feel the sun's glow on his face, to smell the wet earth drying.

The barn was a short walk away. Thick white walls the same as the house's kept it cool in the summer. His mare was already nodding her head in approval as he approached. He stroked her neck and told her the plan for the day. Then attached a bridle and lead, taking her closer to the saddle room. He grabbed the ancient leather saddle, broken in by generations, and hefted it onto her back. Cinching it tight, he brought her out into the sunlight.

"Papa!"

He looked back to the house, seeing his youngest running at him.

"Quiero contigo!"

His eyes found his wife's. Framed in the doorway, she gave him a nod. He picked the boy up and placed him on the front of the saddle. Put a foot into the stirrup and hoisted himself up behind him, groaning from old cornadas as he did so. With a few clicks of his tongue and a light tap from his heels, they set off into the hills.

It was a good ride from the compound to the ganadaria. Through woods and down into the marshier areas. His son tapped his arm to get his attention as they passed a group of wild Iberian pigs. Too engrossed in rooting fallen acorns to care about them.

His son's head bobbed happily from side to side, taking in all the wonder of life emerging after the heavy rains. His own turned on a swivel, eyes moving swiftly, to study the earth, keeping him mindful of the heavy hooved prints all around them that signaled danger. The mare's nose served him well; she caught the scent before he did. She protested slightly as they followed the sickly-sweet smell to its source. There in the muck, about two days dead, was one of the ganadaria's fighting bulls. The massive animal now reduced to carrion food. Upon inspection, he found several cornadas on one side, probably more horn wounds on the other.

He let her steer them a safe distance away, to a hilltop where they could take stock of the herd. Below them, dark shades with glinting horns moved about. The Toros Bravos, the closest descendants left on the planet of the ancient aurochs. The purest form of undomesticated cattle. Bred for their aggressiveness, intelligence, and refusal to be tamed.

Scanning carefully, he took in the animals. Some he knew would be missing. Either dead like the one they found or wandered off to some other area. The four-year-olds were his major concern, closing in at six hundred kilograms, thick muscles toughened by plowing through the mud. He looked for injuries. Which ones had new scars, which were already fighting for dominance, which were lazing around letting cattle egrets eat the flies off them. All of these bulls were kept separate from the females. The only form of tension release they had was to fight. The fighting was good. It honed their massive neck muscles, sharpened their horns. A blood-thirsty pack of herbivores.

From the moment they were born he had tested them. Saw how mere hours out of the womb they were ready to charge. How when they were separated from their mothers and branded, they would stomp the fire, unable to take their pain and rage out on those who did the branding. A few years later, they were tested again by men. On horseback they charged the bulls with blunted lances to see if they could knock them down, to see if they fought. They always fought. Soon more lives would be added to this herd to replace the ones to be sacrificed. Someday his sons would take part in this generational process.

"Murciélago," his son whispered, pointing to the far hill. In full daylight, the massive bull sunned himself, looking down on his own sons. Even from this far distance he could see the scars on the bull's neck. Almost a decade had passed since Murciélago, the unkillable bull, had earned a pardon. That day in the arena the man had stood in front of the bull, cape in hand, and marveled as all of his sword strikes failed to take him down. The crowd, moved by the animal's tenacity, demanded his life be spared. Now he was here, a seed bull ruling over these lands.

"Será uno como Murciélago?" His son's eyes were turned to look at his.

From the other side, Murciélago bellowed a challenge.

"Es posible."

His son knew the truth. What these bulls were ultimately fated for. That in the end they would all face down men like him who would risk their lives with sword and cape to become an arbiter of death. The mighty bulls the symbol of earth, an offering to civilization in the sands of the arena. His boy knew these bulls were destined to die.

He looked across to Murciélago, then patted his son on the head. "Es posible."

It was rare, but it was possible.

# PART ONE
## FREE-RANGE

"Blood is thicker than milk."
—Arab proverb

# CHAPTER 1

0300. THE TACTICAL WATCH ON MICHAEL'S WRIST vibrated from the alarm. The room was black except for the blue digital numbers from the AC unit mounted above the window, its condensation glistening along the thick concrete walls as if he were in the intestines of some great beast. Habit sent his hand to the Beretta M9 resting on the nightstand by his head. Still there. By the time he hit the lights, his pants and boots, though unbuttoned and unlaced, were on. Another habit.

A plywood cross, a poor man's modern version of a Samurai armor stand hammered together, held his helmet and plate carrier, a slimmed-down version of body armor with bullet-proof ceramic plates, sergeant's stripes and his last name—Pilgeram—the only decorations on the camouflage pattern. The whole of it weighed about forty-five pounds with the magazines, smoke grenade, and excess medical gear he liked to keep strapped onto his armor. He threw the kit on over his shoulders and grabbed his helmet, rifle, and aid bag. Most of the items he had, he wouldn't be using on this deployment. Not on this tour.

Outside he jogged to the truck line. The semi-sized mine-resistant vehicles, like some inbred offspring of a tank and a tractor, had already been started up, their low diesel engines grumbling at him as he approached. His truck was third in line; he dropped most of his gear next to the chest-heigh tire on the front passenger side, slung his weapon over his shoulder, then headed over to the gunner's room.

The light of the full moon illuminated the crumbling buildings constructed by the Soviets in the 1970s. They gave Michael an impression of pueblo houses, thick concrete walls that kept cool in the summer. Off to his right stood the more recent American huts that this generation of occupiers had built, wooden boxes that absorbed all heat and cooked those inside.

The majority of the security force advise and assist team that Michael was a part of was billeted on the east side near the gate leading over to the Afghan part of the base. Being the medic, he was housed next to the aid station and had to travel to the rest of the team. Anytime they left on a mission, a short walk took him between the varied buildings. He could just make out what remained of the walls of the British fort from the early 1800s on the other side of the chain-link gate. Beyond the base's surrounding walls, the mountains of Afghanistan punctuated the skyline, glowing in the moonlight like jagged teeth ready to engulf all of them simply by closing its jaws.

Michael entered one of the pueblo-like buildings near the end of the Hesco barriers that encircled them. The gunners all shared a large room that Michael imagined once served as some sort of meeting room for the former Soviet occupiers.

Now it had four beds and jack shacks around the room. Michael found Ned, an unlit cigarette dangling from his lips and a case of Mountain Dew nestled beside him, two items he never seemed to run out of. He went over to Ned's corner to help him grab the big gun. Ned was a really small-framed guy with black hair and black humor. The dude had guts and heart well beyond his stature though. He was the only person on the team that Michael had gone to war with previously.

"Morning, Doc," Ned said, and slammed a half-sized can of a military-issued energy drink. Then, apparently feeling the effects, he heaved the .50-caliber machine gun onto his shoulder.

"Morning, Ned." He grabbed the heavy barrel and its spare, then followed him out to the truck line. Once at the truck, Ned wasted no time in lighting the cigarette hanging from his mouth. Together they began assembling the gun and going through all the function checks. They mounted the gun onto a CROW system, an electronic firing platform that allowed the gunner to stay safely within the vehicle while engaging targets. It came with an adjustable zoom, and night and thermal imaging, giving the Americans more than an unfair advantage in a gunfight. It took a long time to set up and when things failed the gunner had to expose themselves in order to clear or fix the gun, yet it was still safer than sitting on a regular turret. Ned liked to joke that it was too much like a video game. Michael thought he just missed the adrenaline rush that came from the crack and ping of a bullet in comparison to the dull thud when a round did manage to imbed itself in the metal coffin.

Michael lounged in the gunner's seat watching Ned handle the final adjustments, clicking away at the trigger on his commands to ensure that the timing was correct on the .50

cal, critical to avoiding a misfire. Spectacle over, Michael jumped down. "I'm heading to the DFAC. You need anything?"

"Another case of Rip It and maybe some more snacks. Not those fucking muffins either," Ned responded as he lit another cigarette.

Michael passed by the other trucks and took orders for the rest of the team, then walked down to the dining facility to satisfy everyone's orders. He came back with five cases of the energy drinks, a bunch of beef jerky, and plenty of muffins balanced on top of them; he handed these out to all the truck crews, being sure to save an extra couple of muffins for Ned, just to show he cared.

Michael then went around and checked that all the first aid kits, spineboards, and rescue litters were still fully stocked and on their respective trucks. Overkill, maybe. But this way, they'd have everything necessary to deal with an emergency until anyone injured could be evacuated to a higher level of care.

Losing soldiers at this stage, it wouldn't sit well with him. They were already at the decade-plus marker for the War in Afghanistan, and all of the nine non-comms on their sixteen-man team had been on previous deployments. Captain Mallard was the only one of the seven officers to have seen combat. For the rest, this was the last opportunity to distinguish themselves in a war that was on its last rotations, creating a power struggle and an atmosphere of desperation to separate themselves from their peers. Michael couldn't abide it. He saw how it divided the team between those who had deployed and witnessed the true cost of combat, and those in it to make a name for themselves. Meaningless political squabbling. And meanwhile? Their counterparts simply fought and died.

That's not to say that he was overly sympathetic to the Afghan lives being lost. No. He couldn't afford to be. Emotions, he had learned the hard way, didn't mix well on the battlefield. At any time, he might be called upon to treat one of his team. The fact that he wouldn't be able to save everyone, no matter how much he cared... He'd buried that fact, along with his emotions, in some dark recess of his soul. Closed himself off more than most. Compartmentalized. It softened the job, keeping everyone at a distance. Maybe that's how they all did it, at least those who kept coming back.

He did one last preliminary check of his gear before the pre-mission brief, then scored a smoke from Ned, who handed it over with a small frown. Lighting the cigarette, he made his way to the semi-circle that had formed around Captain Mallard. He began going over the mission, how they would be heading north to support the ANA as they conducted a clearing operation in the district. The Afghans would be going house to house, using intel they had gathered to detain suspected insurgents. The team would be assisting solely on the command-and-control front. Not directly engaging with the enemy, not interacting with anyone other than their allies. Everyone already knew the mission and had previously attended a full briefing of the operations order earlier in the week, but Mallard was known for these twice-overs prior to rolling out.

After Captain Mallard finished the overview First Sergeant Porter began with the medical evacuation plan. Porter was Michael's direct boss, a towering ebony figure standing a head taller than anyone else on the team and broader than them all. He was responsible for this portion of the plan but

Michael had written and developed the majority of it, so instead of listening, he looked for who was paying attention. Most, not surprisingly, were fully tuned into this portion of the briefing; also not surprising was who wasn't. The same egocentric ones who relished stirring up drama.

He sighed inwardly. There was nothing he could do to make them see things his way. All he could do was prepare himself for the worst.

Thirty minutes until dawn and the excuses were already pouring in. As usual the Afghans were not on schedule. It would still be another hour before they left.

Staff Sergeant Pupalia, their intelligence specialist, laughingly called out over the radio, "Wouldn't want to catch the Taliban off guard!" That had some truth to it, but mostly it came down to morning prayer. They were always at odd ends when it came to culture; the Americans hard-charging and unfailingly military-oriented in their objectives, the Afghans devoted to their religion and family-first mindset.

True to habit, the Afghan army began leaving the compound about thirty minutes after sunrise. The team in their four trucks followed soon after. Michael slouched down, letting his head lean forward with the weight of his helmet to squeeze in some rest during the trek out to the first location. Ned was on the gun above, rocking out to some heavy metal music playing through the headsets they all wore. Porter sat in the passenger seat, serving as traffic controller, and Lieutenant Harris, their communications officer, was driving. Michael drifted off to sleep in the back fairly quickly, letting the music of the engine and the rumble of Five Finger Death Punch lure him to sleep.

# CHAPTER 2

*"Word from the interpreter is that we got several wounded,"* Captain Mallard voiced over the radio.

*"Roger. Hang tight until it gets sorted."* An unfamiliar voice, mostly likely from the battalion operations center.

*"Roger. Out."*

It'd been about forty-five minutes. The radio chatter that'd woken him now had his teammates interrupting the rock ballads in his ear.

"Jesus Christ these guys are fucking brilliant, aren't they?" First Sergeant Porter let out. "Hang fucking tight until it gets sorted. Great advice, asshole."

"Am I up?" Michael asked.

Porter looked back at him from his seat. "Well, good fucking morning. And no, as per usual, nobody knows what the fuck is happening."

"Cool, I'll go back to sleep, then."

"Not yet. From the sounds of it, these assholes got fucked to hell. No number yet, but more than likely they'll be coming to you."

Michael cracked open an energy drink. "Want us to go check it out? Might be fun, good practice for me."

"Nah, these guys need to learn to sort out their own shit. Their medics need to do their fucking job and I don't need you away from us."

Michael slowed his chugging of the precious caffeine down to a steady sip. "Whatever you say, boss."

Turned out a Ford Ranger hit an IED and flipped. The report they got over the radio was that the driver was killed instantly, the two passengers severely injured. The Afghan medics had them stabilized and, as predicted, were coming back this way. They would try to get the Americans to use their air assets to evacuate the injured. Michael knew the medical rules of engagement. They could only offer aviation support if the Afghan soldier was on a supporting mission with coalition forces. If Michael decided the casualties needed urgent medical care in order to survive their wounds, they'd get their helicopter ride to an American trauma hospital. But it would have to be approved and debated several echelons above him first. Even if the assets were available, more than likely it wouldn't be approved. The drawdown dictated that they didn't need to provide any higher level of care than what they could administer at the local level.

"Time to go to work, Doc," Porter said now that he'd shared the situation update.

"Alright, boss, I'm hopping out to see where I can examine these bros." With that, Michael dropped the back of the ramp with a *hiss* from its pneumatic plungers and hit the dirt.

He had taken notice of the terrain after he had woken up but began reassessing now that he was on the ground. Mentally he mapped out where he could land a helicopter and where he could stage and assess the injured beforehand. He chose a compound abutting the road to the west of their position. There was good surrounding cover—several trucks and a low wall about hip-high—and access to grass fields on the far side. It was open enough for the team to easily secure and tall enough that if bullets started flying, he could duck out of sight. The sun was still pretty low and would be to their backs, so anyone looking in their direction from the far side would be blind to what they were doing.

He keyed the hand mic on his radio. "7, 7. Mike. I think we got a good spot here."

"Roger, I'm coming out," came the grumble from Porter. "All available dismounts meet at Doc's location." He got out of the truck and lumbered over to Michael's position. He took stock of it, nodded like a proud father, then went about putting the trucks and other team members in a defensive posture for the area.

Captain Mallard then walked over. On his left was his interpreter, Jawees; on his right, Afghan army commander Rhamaanigul. The man was screaming into his radio and at Captain Mallard simultaneously, hands flaring about no matter which he was addressing. Behind them came the entire entourage for Rhamaanigul along with several other young officers trying to do their part. Captain Mallard had himself a balancing act between trying to keep them on mission and showing that he cared about their casualties.

"How we doing, Doc?"

"Ready, sir, but can I borrow Jawees when they come in?"

"No problem. Anything else?"

"Yeah, sir, I'm going to need you to clear out this gaggle when the wounded come in. You know how they get."

"I'll do my best on that part."

Just then the Afghan ambulance, converted from an older model American Humvee, pulled up and chaos ensued. Michael grabbed Jawees. "Hey, go over there and tell the medics to bring them into that walled compound," he said while pointing. "Then tell the rest of them to fuck off out of here while I do my job."

"Okay, boss," Jawees said, and began unloading on the crowd in high-speed Pashtun.

Captain Mallard and Michael stood back to let the Afghan medics relocate the wounded. Jawees had no effect on the crowd, which was only growing with their unnecessary effort to help the medics. Once they got the first one moving to the spot Michael had designated, he matched their pace to look the guy over. He exchanged his gloves for disposable ones to safeguard himself against the blood. The Afghan was peppered with shrapnel, mostly on his left side, and had abrasions on his head. Their medics had done a fairly good job of bandaging him up; only a few spots needed to be readjusted and covered. Michael was semi-proud of himself—these were the Afghan medics he had trained.

"*JAWEES!*" he screamed, getting the interpreter's attention. "Tell the guys they did a good job, but they need to readjust the bandage on his leg. It's a little too loose and sliding down. Also have one of them start an IV on his right arm."

"Okay, Doc."

As Jawees started off in Pashtun again, Michael jogged over to the second casualty, in the process of being lowered down . This guy must have been the gunner. Almost all his wounds were on his upper body where areas would have been exposed if he had been in a turret. His upper lip was curled up and in, parts of the jawbone exposed. Shrapnel and dirt speckled his cheeks and chest. His head was wrapped in a loose bandage that had an interesting pinkish tint to it instead of an arterial bright red or dark venous crimson. His breathing was rasp and erratic—agonal breathing. The guy was fucked.

The Afghan medics finished lowering him to the ground and Michael unwrapped the bandage on his head partway. He was looking directly at a still-living brain. Carefully he wrapped it back up.

Captain Mallard, standing over him, cringed. "What do you need, Doc?"

"Well, sir, this guy is fucked. The other dude over there I'd list as a priority for evac. This guy urgent surgical." He sat back on his heels. *I finally get to try this.* "I'm going to do a cricothyroidotomy."

"Does he need it?"

"Yes and no. I could use the practice either way." He already had his aid bag on the ground and rummaged in it for his cric kit. He unrolled the kit across the wounded Afghan's chest like a master chef unrolling his knife set. Michael started by cleaning the intended incision area below the Adam's apple with an alcohol pad. He grabbed the scalpel, uncovered the blade from its plastic sheath, and cut a vertical line about an inch long, using two fingers from his offhand to spread the wound open and expose the white membrane underneath the skin, capillary blood slowly pooling in the cut. He punctured the membrane with the blade, flipped the scalpel around, and twisted the dull end in the first incision to fully open the larynx as though cracking open an oyster. Using curved mosquito clamps he dilated the hole in the membrane and slipped the cut tube in just past the balloon cuff. With a 5 mL syringe, he inflated the balloon to secure it in place. The casualty's response was automatic; finally he was able to achieve a breath of air through the tube. Blood and mucus spouted forcefully all over Michael from the new airway.

"Well, that was lovely." Still, with the spray of the casualty's lung fluids all over him, he was confident that the tube was placed correctly, and finished securing it with tape.

"Might want to rinse your mouth out, Doc," Mallard said with a grotesque look.

Without responding to Captain Mallard, Michael asked, "Is the 9-line up? Are they getting a bird?"

Captain Mallard had his head cocked to listen to his hand-mic. "Porter sent it about five minutes ago; still no word back."

Michael nodded, checked back in on the first casualty, and instructed the medics on additional care for the other. He really was happy with the progress that they were making. They genuinely cared about the job and their skills were improving.

After thirty minutes had passed, Captain Mallard walked back over. "No bird, Doc."

"What? Really?"

"Apparently this mission isn't joint enough to qualify

according to our higher-ups. These guys are going to have to drive them back to their aid station."

"Well, ain't that some shit." Michael grabbed his bag and went back to his truck.

# CHAPTER 3

THE MISSION WENT BACK TO NORMAL. BORING FOR Michael. He swapped seats with Ned in the gunner's chair to let him get some rest. The two rotated like this until the Afghans had enough intel or prisoners or good will spread amongst the townsfolk that they could return from patrol. From start to finish the whole operation took over sixteen hours.

Back at the FOB the team downloaded their gear, cleaned out the trucks, refueled, and reset every piece of equipment they would need if they had to go back out at a moment's notice. For Michael this meant assisting Ned with breaking down the .50-cal. Ned always cleaned the gun after every patrol; even though the only rounds he'd put through it were for his test fires, he'd kept the discipline and hard-earned lessons from past deployments. Better to leave as little to chance when it came to a gunfight.

After the truck was set and the gun down, Michael went to the aid station to refill his aid bag, putting together another cric kit from spare parts. He met up with Ned and the other junior NCOs on their way to dinner chow. Besides Michael, only three other guys held E5 rank on the team: Ned, Luke, and Dusten. One-on-one, they were fun guys to hang around. All three of them in the room was pure entertainment.

"Hola, amigos."

"What's up, Doc?" All. Almost in unison.

"Heard you were slitting throats like a savage today," Luke said, bringing his hand across his throat.

"Heard you were beating your dick in the turret for fourteen hours straight."

"I was hoping we'd get shot at so I could get in a combat jack. Had to settle for splooging into Kalian's supersized Kevlar." He leaned in, feigning a grimace an inch from Ned's cheek. Ned pushed him off, his palm flat against his stupid face.

Lieutenant Kalian embodied the worst aspects you could ask for in a leader. He'd brought the team under scrutiny by pitting the higher-ups against each other, usurping Captain Mallard's authority. It was bad enough that the captain had to pander between multitudes of people forcefully dictating how and when the team would do its job—and oftentimes issuing contradicting commands and guidance. Lieutenant Kalian had chosen to stir that pot and exploit it. Michael's point of view was, he was just crying about not going out enough to earn a Combat Badge or gain some form of notoriety with his seniors. His little mutiny had earned the team unneeded eyeballs on them.

"How the fuck is someone with that big of a head that fucking stupid?" Luke asked. "I mean, how did his parents not smother him?"

"People like him are the reason Planned Parenthood exists," Dusten said, fiddling with the safety on his rifle.

"I feel bad that you have to ride in the same truck as him," Michael said to Luke.

"Tell me stupid isn't contagious, Doc."

Dusten frowned. "Doc's probably going to have to check your dick for STDs."

"I bet you couldn't even find it after you shot it into that big ol' bucket," Ned added, snickering.

Dinner that evening was chicken cordon bleu, which was served at least twice a week, along with the usual duo of butter noodles and green peas with carrots. With the draw-down, they were down to one hot meal a day throughout the deployment. Every chance they got, they had lunch with the Afghans just for a change of flavor.

Food in front of them, the four ate quickly and for the most part quietly. Conversation usually came at the end of the meal when everyone was done eating. The chow hall did have a TV, but it only got one channel, the Armed Forces Network. They watched as news of the Boston Marathon bombing aired.

Michael pointed, almost blasting Dusten in the nose. "Look at that dude! He put on what actually looks like an effective improvised tourniquet!"

Luke nudged him. "Fucking nerd."

"Unarmed innocent civilians get blown up, you're hard over a scrap of cloth," Dusten added, stone-faced.

"Yeah, keep your nads in check," Ned chimed in.

"Sweet Jesus, you guys are assholes," Michael breathed out.

"Whoa, you can't bring Jesus into it, Doc," Dusten said, face serious. "Ned's people kinda killed him. It's just not right."

Luke joined him. "What did Jesus do to you people anyway, Ned?"

Ned looked thoughtful for a moment, then said, "You needed someone to die for your sins. You're welcome."

Michael rolled his eyes. "Nobody's letting that sacrifice go in vain at this table."

Luke nudged him again. "Do you think helmet skeet is a sin, Doc?"

# CHAPTER 4

After dinner Michael went back to his room to relax for a bit. On his makeshift dresser next to the crude armor stand was a cheap humidor half-filled with cigars that he had gotten online and delivered to Afghanistan. After every mission, his higher-ups gathered for a cigar session and discussed the team's progression. Michael was the lowest ranking person allowed at their table and enjoyed his status as part of the decision-making process. Everyone attended the daily meeting, but it was these informal cigar sessions that most impacted what direction they'd all take. What was the next course of action, venting about the different issues they were having, bullshitting and airing out their complaints about the army or problems with spouses or significant others. In other words, a bunch of guys grabbing a beer after work, just with a job with more serious consequences.

Next to Michael's cigar box was an unpainted tin canteen. It was filled with Irish whiskey that his family smuggled to him inside mouthwash bottles. He let his food digest for a bit before he took a long pull from the bottle. It had only been several hours since they had returned from the mission, and he let the whiskey loosen up his shoulders and neck as it slid down his throat. That part of his body was always tense after long missions of wearing the helmet, and the years of that weight bearing down on his spine wasn't helping it any. A couple minutes later, that familiar haze sifted through his brain, relaxing him. He flicked through the cigar box, which held a few souvenirs he'd collected on this tour along with an aluminum memorial bracelet that he'd kept safe from his first. He picked a cigar out. Grabbed his 9mm pistol. Headed out the door.

The senior leaders were already sitting down when Michael got to the spot a couple of buildings away. Captain Mallard and First Sergeant Porter had already lit their cigars. Staff Sergeant Pupalia was sitting on the opposite side of the table from them, his cigar occasionally casting a glow back onto his glasses and setting his eyes aflame like a demon librarian. On the same bench was Sergeant First Class Conchord and then there was First Lieutenant Hektar, the executive officer and the second-in-command. Tall, athletic, a natural leader. Michael saw him as one of the rare charismatic types that people naturally wanted to follow. He and Conchord were the ones involved in helping the Afghans develop their planning and operations.

Captain Mallard exhaled a deep puff into the air as Michael took a seat at the end of the table next to Porter. "The Afghans will be holding a memorial service for the two guys they lost today. Tomorrow at 0900; as usual we'll all be there."

"How did they take the fact that we wouldn't evacuate them?" Michael asked, taking his cigar out and casually cutting it.

"This will weaken Rhamaanigul's position with his men, he says. The executive officer and the spiritual officer seemed to have taken it in stride. I tried to apologize but they shrugged their shoulders. Inshallah and all that."

"Those two know how this goes," Conchord said, gesturing with his cigar. "Both of them fought with the Russians when they controlled the country. I had a nice long chat with them about that the other day. They said they are preparing for when we leave. Wouldn't lose sleep over it, Doc." He leaned in, dropping the ash from his cigar into an empty ammo can in the middle of the table. "At least you got some practice in," he said with a grin that pulled taut all the cords in his over-sized neck.

Michael nodded and lit his cigar. He hadn't expected anything different. "Yeah, I guess I did," he said as footsteps approached from around the corner.

Lieutenant Kalian appeared uninvited and loitered at the end of the table. He seemed not to notice the change in mood. "Heard that guy was pretty much dead by the time you started working on him."

Michael studied the lit end of his cigar for a moment before replying. "Yeah, you could say that. What's your point?"

"Don't you think that's a little messed up? Misuse of medical resources? What you did, that's like using another human being as a guinea pig. That weigh on you at all, or no?"

Captain Mallard stood. "Look, Brigade has nowhere else to put your sorry ass, so I'm stuck keeping you. But you should really start thinking about the bridges burning behind you. Unless you want an enemy out of everyone on this post, I suggest you walk away. Might also consider how it might be a good idea to keep the person responsible for your life happy and on your side."

Kalian looked at Michael. "No hard feelings, Doc."

Michael didn't respond; he was more concerned with the smoke drifting off of the end of his cigar.

Kalian had started to walk away when Michael called out to him. "Sir."

Kalian turned back, looking almost hopeful.

"I showed our Afghan allies that I was trying to save their friend's life. So what if I view it as practice? Would you rather I pop my cherry cutting your throat one day? Or do you think you can appreciate my detachment from humanity as someone who might benefit from it one day?" Michael held a stare as Kalian slowly disengaged and turned around, the group watching as he turned the dark corner.

"You know what's inhumane to me?" Conchord said after a few minutes. "The fact that we have to keep that mouth-breathing oxygen thief here. That's inhumane."

Pupalia adjusted his glasses. "You'd think after being shot down for the drama he's already caused that he'd sit down and shut up. What do you think, Doc? Some kind of personality disorder?"

Michael smiled at that. "Case of the stupid more like. Question for the college grads here: How the fuck does he have a degree?"

"He's a political science major," said Hektar. "Barely counts."

"Judging by his actions on this team, he should have failed the shit out of that."

That brought a round of laughter to the table. Even Mallard cracked a smile. Michael took a long drag and leaned back against the concrete wall behind him. A bit of ash dropped from his cigar as he gestured. "People on high like to play fuck-fuck games with us on the bottom, so we're left with someone who turned his back on the command structure."

It didn't help that Kalian was a favorite of someone at the brigade level either; especially with the ongoing friction between Mallard and Captain Behorde, their garrison commander and a notorious hard-ass, that left Kalian an opening to exploit. Behorde and Mallard were the highest-ranking officers on the outpost, and often at odds. Mallard's team was there to support the Afghan army they shared the base with, while Captain Behorde's charge was base security. He saw it as owning a battle space, and he held that over Captain Mallard as often as he could. To make matters even more complicated, both commanders each had their own bosses they had to report to. Who in turn played out the drama of the two captains on a larger scale. The seeds of sedition sown by Lieutenant Kalian had been planted in that ongoing struggle.

Sergeant Porter grinned at Michael. "Just wait until you get to our level, Doc. You'll learn to love the fuckery. Learn to nod along and collect your fucking paycheck."

"No thanks, I'm done. They've killed the fun. I thought I'd joined a brutal fighting force but I'm a cog in some political machine."

Porter leaned in toward him. "What makes you think anything's different from before? Only difference is now you're getting a peek behind the curtain."

Hektar spoke up. "This is why I'm getting out of the regular army. It's off to Special Forces I go after this tour. If I have to play this game, it won't be this political shit we're playing right now."

Michael knew instantly that he would sail through the grueling selection process. Wouldn't help though. "Oh, you'll end up back here, and working the politics of this region," Michael said. "We may be packing up, but the chance of this being done is zero. I don't think we can ever completely abandon Afghanistan. Even if it is a country with no real borders or united culture, this"—he gestured to the landscape—"is about as united as the North and South Poles."

"At least it'll be fun, Doc. Change can happen, but not this way."

Captain Mallard sat back. "I agree with Hektar, Doc. Takes a different machine and more time."

Conchord smiled. "Forget the nation-building. I don't know why we haven't turned this whole place into one big training area. We come over, fuck shit up, keep our boys sharp. Now that would be a productive use of this country."

First Sergeant Porter laughed. "What makes you think that's not what we're already doing?"

# CHAPTER 5

"I REALLY SHOULDN'T BE DOING THIS," MICHAEL SAID AS HE laid his supplies out on Conchord's dresser. He had followed him to his room after their cigars. They had a bi-weekly ritual.

"Don't get moral qualms about this now. You know I'd just do it myself."

"I know, but this is going to fuck you in the long run."

Conchord was pushing forty, and the abuse to his body was wearing him down. The man already had two purple hearts; one because of the shrapnel in his left side from when he was knocked out by the enemy's nearby mortar round, the other from a gunshot wound to his left leg sustained in Iraq. Michael had been there for the mortar blast. The man was forever changed by the traumatic brain injury, occasionally taking on the demeanor of a punch-drunk boxer, a lost look in his eyes. Even when he wasn't one hundred percent, he was still one of the best NCOs he had ever worked with.

"The long run?" Conchord scoffed. "I need to not be fucked *now*. I have a job to do, and I need every edge I can get. To include your steady hand. You know as well as I do there's no such thing as a fair fight."

"Might be time to close shop and start looking for life elsewhere."

"Are you really getting out?" Conchord asked as he pulled his pants down, exposing the upper portion of a butt cheek.

"Yup." Michael responded by drawing the black-market steroids into the syringe. "It feels like life is herding me into civilization."

"I think it's a mistake."

Michael moved over and cleaned the area with an alcohol swab. "Do you think I want to do this shit for the rest of my life?" he asked as he plunged the needle into Conchord's ass and pushed the stopper until the chamber was empty.

Conchord didn't flinch. "You know you love it out here as much as I do."

"Hanging around a bunch of sweaty dudes nonstop. Little brown people constantly trying to kill me. Allies who don't know fuck from what they're doing and a government with bigger issues stateside than any of the shit we're dealing with out here?" Michael put a band-aid over the puncture site. "Sorry, brother, but I'm going to use the benefits I got before that government decides that veterans have had enough funding."

Conchord pulled up his pants and turned to look him in the eye. "That won't happen. Can't piss off the only people who actually know how to fight. You know it's going to suck out there, right? Here we dominate, free to be wild, the alpha males God intended us to be. You go back home—to where? California? You'll be lost in a sea of liberalism."

"What's the alternative? This doesn't feel like we're on top. Hiding behind the Afghans and letting them take the fight to the enemy." Michael grew quiet for a minute and stared at Conchord's body armor resting on its stand. "This is the only thing I've done since turning eighteen. Dude, if something's going to change, I have to do it now. Otherwise, I'm doing this for the rest of my life."

"Would that be so bad?" Conchord smiled at him and dropped a hand on his shoulder. "Guys like us? We're cursed by the thrill we get being out here. You'll forever be chasing this high. Trust me."

Michael shrugged. "You can't be doing this forever. Hell, the fact that I'm juicing you up is a sign that it's going to have to end for you at some point."

Conchord's eyes went blank. "I don't even want to think about it, Doc. I'm a lifer, you know that." His eyes, too, drifted to his body armor. "I really am cursed, you know? There's no use for me back in the States."

The quiet that filled the space in the room concerned Michael. "How's your head doing? Still getting migraines?"

The question pulled Conchord out of his staring contest with the armor stand. "Migraines, constant ringing in my ears. Drives me crazy." He looked at Michael. "Don't worry about me, Doc. You're keeping me here doing what I was meant to do."

Michael sighed. "Tell the medic not to worry. Yeah, sure."

# CHAPTER 6

It was almost midnight. He was tired but his mind was running, so he walked. He thought about getting out, about going to college. He thought about women. Women! Something he hadn't really experienced since the heartbreak of love lost on his first deployment. It'd forced the dawn of his misogynistic, sexist attitude, one he could feel expanding as he watched every shit relationship in the army, further uncoupling him from humanity. The few people he knew with healthy, stable relationships gave him hope, but little of it. In the world he lived in, there was an excess of divorce that seemed to be the main supply of bodies for the war machine.

He wandered around the inner perimeter of the post. Contemplated calling his family. He knew how that conversation would go. No matter who he called they would ask him if he was okay, if he was safe, if he was doing well. In these cases, he always told them what they needed to hear. The truth of the situation was far too wild for their civilized minds to comprehend. He knew his father would make him feel guilty for being over here. His mother was off traveling somewhere in the world; she'd be encouraging, but hard to get a hold of. So, at peace with his excuses, he kept walking.

Before he knew it, he was on the other end of the base. The gate to the Afghan side and the helipad beyond it stood before him. At least one American and an Afghan security guard, well paid for his loyalty, always guarded it. Michael walked through the gate with a shoddy explanation. Technically he wasn't supposed to go over alone. However, late-night emergencies happened all the time. Those assigned this shift had learned to accept this, and let him pass.

On the other side of the helipad loomed the ruins of the British fort. Michael didn't know when exactly it was built, only that it stood during the latter stages of the British empire as it tried to control Afghanistan. They had come with rifles to this part of the world with conscripts from modern-day India and Pakistan. Had expected to gain control of the Khyber Pass and thus dominate the silk trade. The archaic mud walls stood ten meters high and still showed signs of battle, even these hundreds of years later. The Russian-made buildings were a stone's throw away from this. Another historical marker. In a couple hundred years the American buildings would serve as another artifact of a foreign occupier if they weren't torn down completely. A question Michael often thought about was whether the American occupiers would be overrun and slaughtered like those who came before them. Yet another invader the Afghans denied.

A smile slid onto his face. He tilted it up to the full moon, its light supercharging him. His hand moved down to touch the pistol on his hip. Maybe Conchord was right. He did love this feeling. The simplicity. He either survived or he didn't. There were no worries beyond that.

Maybe he was cursed too. More than enough blood had spilled on this ground for some ancient blood ritual to have completed, the thousands of years of sacrifice on this soil enough to follow any invader anywhere they might go in the world as a stain on their souls.

Standing in defiance in the moonlight, Michael stood strong and enjoyed the moment. A land devoted to the God of War, ruins built upon ruins.

# PART TWO
# THE RUN

*"Peace is only better than war when it's not hell too. War being hell makes sense."*
—Walker Percy

# CHAPTER 7

Michael was sitting in his used four-wheel drive truck loaded with everything he owned just outside the out-processing center at Fort Campbell, Kentucky. A piece of paper on his passenger seat stared him down. Michael picked up the DD214, a summary of his military life. The only life he'd ever known, really. Duty stations, deployments overseas, schools attended, awards and ranks achieved. Total time in uniform, months shy of a decade. Now all of those years, all of the bullets and blood, had come to an end, taking form as a single sheet of paper. For most, he imagined that this moment was a happy occasion. On social media he had seen others who had gotten out, most with much fewer years of service, literally clicking their heels with excitement over this moment. He had felt that way too for a brief second.

An icy hand wrapped around his heart, squeezing out the memory of that drop of happiness and driving him to panic. In the rearview mirror, he looked stone-faced, like nothing was wrong. Inside, he was in turmoil. Had he made a mistake?

What would he do now? He belonged *here*, on a base. Would he belong back home? Was it still home?

His hand shook, his breaths quickened. He looked around the cab of the truck for something, anything to stop the panic. Then he remembered his collection of alcohol, packed in a box on the back seat. Reaching back, he pulled out the first bottle that he could reach. An expensive Irish whiskey that he had picked up on his way through Shannon, Ireland, after leaving Afghanistan, one he'd planned on saving, on savoring, in the right moment. He pulled the wooden cork out and took several long pulls. The alcohol would numb him. Emotions had tried to creep in on him before in between deployments, but a little drink to refocus his eyes on the mission ahead always helped keep them away. Nothing like this—like this *fear*—had happened to him before. But the drink still did the trick, calming his breathing, steadying his shaking hand, releasing the cold grip on his heart.

He took two deep breaths. Pushed his forehead into the steering wheel. Closed his eyes.

He was still on post, in a parking lot outside of the out-processing facility, a bottle in his hand.

He had to get away.

He carefully returned the bottle to the box behind his seat. Started the engine. Put it in drive.

The truck bumped toward the gate to the civilian world. After passing the guard station, he turned onto the main road.

He couldn't help himself. He glanced back at the unit emblems displayed on the tall walls that enclosed Fort Campbell.

# CHAPTER 8

Michael felt like he had been let loose from the safety of those high walls and sent off on his own for the first time. He plotted a course through the southern half of the United States, one that would pass through San Antonio and Las Vegas to see family—his uncles on his father's side, who had also served in the military. He hadn't seen any of them since he enlisted but had stayed in contact through phone calls, letters, and care packages. Stopping by their houses would at least mean a warm bed for a night and a decent meal. A welcome change from sleeping in his truck as he got himself back to California.

The trip did not bring the expected nostalgia, the sense of a return to reality. He drove, impassive, through western Tennessee, passing through Memphis with its giant modern pyramid. He had heard that the building had been converted into a sporting goods megastore. With the mood he was in, he didn't want to be around a bunch of strange people trying to find entertainment.

After Memphis the land turned barren, with very few topographic features to distract him from the thousands of miles he had left. He passed through Little Rock without any hesitation and entered West Texas. After these ten-plus hours, the wear of the road was taking hold of him, and he had to pull over at a rest stop just past Dallas to keep from nodding off.

Still, sleep eluded him, his mind wandering. He absently picked up one of the large files underneath the DD214 and flipped through it. Medical records. The file had grown thicker in the past year, fed by the encouragement of his peers to acknowledge every ache and pain, to have it documented by his doctors. There was a twinge of pride mixed with his guilt over this. For years he had put off seeing anyone about any pain he was experiencing, self-medicating with booze and antihistamines. Yet even when his long list of diagnoses grew, he'd accomplished so much. He wasn't entirely sure if the pride stemmed from keeping himself together despite all they diagnosed or from the fact that he was still standing at all.

The guilty feeling, he didn't understand it at all.

Maybe it came from knowing that there were guys far worse off than he was. Broken backs. Cancer. Missing limbs. PTSD to the point where they couldn't leave their own houses. PTSD to the point where they killed themselves. Not to mention those who didn't even get the chance to come home. While he had been told that he had earned these things, he couldn't stop comparing himself to them. Couldn't stop feeling selfish. The problem was, he didn't know that much about himself outside of being a soldier. What might his life look like had he never gone this route? What would his life be now without the combat and discipline?

He turned the page in the file and studied the diagnostic sheet that listed everything wrong with him. Most of them tied directly to an active military lifestyle. To long marches hauling a heavy pack over rough terrain. To years of hitting the gym and running fifty-plus miles a week.

The list felt exaggerated. He had all the aches and pains, sure, but he still had an athletic build.

Only one caught his eye and held his attention. The compressed vertebrae at the base of his neck. That constant dull ache. He put the folder back on the seat and tried to relax. Rubbed the back of his neck. Reached for a bottle, this time choosing a cheaper brand.

All the years of wearing a helmet, all the strain that had built up his neck and shoulder muscles. Possibly the pain was from something worse.

# CHAPTER 9

THE NEXT MORNING MICHAEL GOT UP AND BRUSHED HIS teeth in the rest stop bathroom. He checked his GPS to see how long it would take to reach San Antonio. After confirming that he had about another five hours to drive with stops for food and gas, he got into his truck and started driving.

San Antonio was a city well known to him. Immediately following basic training, he'd been sent to Fort Sam Houston near the city's center. Dubbed Whiskeytown, it was the place where the United States Army trained all of its combat medics, the premier first responders to trauma anywhere in the world.

He'd made a lot of fun memories here as a young man sneaking into bars with the older trainees. The place had an almost luxurious feel to it, as the barracks abutted the post's golf course. However, the barracks themselves, shaped like giant concrete spaceships, were the opposite of luxurious.

Yes, he had trained hard here and had played hard as well. He laughed to himself recalling drunken moments in downtown San Antonio where he and his friends purposely mispronounced *Aye-lame-o* to piss off the locals. It never really worked. The people in the area were huge supporters of the military. They could easily overlook the drunken shenanigans of a few kids and happily invited them in. The level of support and love he got here was something he'd never forget. A time of innocence and ignorance to the job he had committed his life to.

These thoughts had him grinning as he drove up to his uncle's suburban home in the city's outskirts. He pulled in alongside the driveway, and before he could get out of the vehicle, his uncle was already striding from the house to greet him. Feet from his truck, Michael found himself embraced in a bear hug.

His Uncle Sam would never leave San Antonio. A larger-than-life man retired from the service, he was a classic embodiment of the Corps. Big and tall, and looking a lot less athletic these days, but once a Marine, always a Marine, and he carried his decades of service with pride.

"Welcome to Texas, soldier!" Sam gripped Michael's palm in a powerful handshake, nodding at the bracelet he wore.

"Thanks," Michael said with an awkward smile. "It's good to be back."

"I'm sure it is. Come on in, get yourself cleaned up. Afterward, your Auntie Maria and I want to treat you to dinner."

"That sounds good. Thank you." Michael grabbed his small travel bag and stepped onto the front porch, where his aunt greeted him with a Texas-sized hug and kiss.

"It is so good to see you, Michael."

"Great to see you too! Thanks for all the care packages you sent throughout the years. I really appreciated every one of them."

"You think nothing of it. We were so proud to be able to support you while you were over there," she cooed in her Mexican accent. Her voice went a little lower. "And your cousin, who's still back over there." She smiled at him, motherly worry behind her eyes. "Now go inside and make yourself comfortable."

Michael set his stuff down in the guest bedroom and went into the bathroom. It took a couple of minutes to peel himself away from his reflection, remembering he still had family deployed to Afghanistan and wishing for a moment he was back there doing what he knew how to do. He splashed some cold water on his face, trying to scare away the anxiety.

Once showered and dressed and standing stiffly in the living room, his uncle and aunt suggested they leave for dinner. They went to a franchise bar and grill close to their home. Michael, unsure of what they might think of his drinking habits, hesitated before ordering a shot of whiskey with his beer.

Sam frowned. "You know you won't find any answers with that," he said to Michael as his aunt ordered a glass of sweet tea.

Michael nodded. "I guess I'm not so much looking for answers as I am trying to forget the question."

"Be careful there. It can take over you, trust me."

He'd forgotten until now the few stories his dad had shared about the trouble Sam had gotten into.

"I've been sober for five years, and my life has never been better."

Maria took Sam's hand in solidarity.

Not knowing what to say, Michael nodded again, and after a few moments without speaking Sam commented on the aluminum band on Michael's right wrist that was stamped with the name, unit, and date of death of a service member. The guy was the first wounded soldier to die on him. Michael was there when the soldier's lights went out, unable to perform any treatment for the gunshot to the head that had him dead seconds after he'd hit the ground. Michael had tenderly taken care of his remains until they could evacuate the body. He always felt weird when people asked. Sometimes he didn't think himself worthy of wearing it—he'd barely known him, hadn't been connected to him in life—but he felt naked without it. Like a piece of his personality and the actions in his life that defined him as a man would be taken away if he ever took it off.

He did his best to explain it. His aunt and uncle went silent for a while. He didn't know how to read that.

# CHAPTER 10

After dinner they went back to the house. His aunt fussed over him by preparing the guest bedroom. She got everything as perfect for him as it could be, then excused herself and went to bed. Sam, still awake, brought him out to the living room. He poured him a glass of tea that he said was the best in Okinawa. Fox News played in the background as they sat and sipped.

A new story popped up on the screen. The one about the only American prisoner of war brought back to the United States after the current administration traded five Taliban commanders for him the previous year. It was an extremely controversial move, as everyone in the military regarded this person not as a POW but as a deserter. Michael, well-aware of the situation, listened in disgust as the news talked about his homecoming. The guy had walked away from his unit and got captured. Had, Michael believed, made himself a political pawn for the Haqqani network.

"Can you believe this shit?" his uncle growled. "Calling this piece of shit a hero."

"He's a fucking deserter and deserves to be shot," Michael said, clenching his glass of tea. "I don't care about his reasons. He committed the ultimate sin in combat. He walked away from his brothers. There is no justification for that."

"It's this fucking president's fault. He is completely fucking this country up. Everything he's doing is pissing on the Constitution. Everything. Play nice and hope for the best. These left-wing liberals have no idea what this country is all about. They're trying to destroy the Constitution. And that fucking asshole of a president is the one leading this country into hell."

The insults to the president discomfited Michael. He didn't have any love for man—in fact, his experiences in Afghanistan and the mistakes he saw from the administration angered him. However, he didn't enjoy the level of disrespect that had grown throughout the country, the ease with which people bad-mouthed their president. Even if justified. There was a level of respect Michael still carried for the office from the previous administration, and he didn't agree with everything they had done either. He couldn't help seeing the dramatic shift in ideology from when he first left. It worried him, but he still maintained a soldier's discipline of not insulting the commander in chief. That's not to say that there were others in the military who didn't. "I'm not sure if you can blame the president; it's not like Congress is effecting any significant change."

Sam barely controlled himself. "That's bullshit. Congress is shit too, but that man is *commander in chief*! My son, your cousin, is in Helmand right now because these imbeciles are willing to send boys like you and him over there and then tie their hands behind their backs by announcing a withdrawal.

I'll blame the president for all he deserves. As the saying goes, the buck stops with him."

"That's true." Michael thought about his cousin and everyone else who was still deployed. Remembered his own frustration when he was over there and the withdrawal announced. The distrust in their Afghan allies as they tried to set them up for success. They must have also seen the withdrawal notice as abandonment. It seemed lazy to blame it on one person. There was something deeper to the faults in the government. Michael just didn't know where the blame fully landed and chose not to respond.

His uncle got up and refilled their tea, and they carried on watching the news for a while in silence. The stock market had increased, unemployment sitting at an all-time low since the recession hit. "At least the economy is doing good."

A curious, angry glance from his uncle. "Good for who? Every time a democrat slips into office, a whole new level of despotism enters into law, manufacturing gets shipped overseas, and more taxes get piled onto the working class. They're chipping away at our God-given rights, listed right there in the Constitution." Sam thrust his pointer finger down into the arm of his chair as though a copy sat there. "The problem with all these politicians is they think they can regulate the humanity right out of society while they line their own pockets." They both stared at the television. Slowly they finished their glasses. As Sam tilted the last bit down his throat, he looked over at Michael. "Are you registered as a republican?"

Michael hesitated, the pressure of his uncle steering him toward the right a weight. "Honestly, Uncle Sam," he said, rubbing the back of his neck, "I haven't thought about the politics back here. Been a little busy on the sharp end of it."

"It's something you should think about," Uncle Sam said, nodding at Michael. "You're heading back to California, and God knows that state needs some true American values flowing back into it." He studied his empty cup for a bit. "Don't think your duty to this country ends because you no longer wear the uniform."

Michael did have some obligation, but to what extent? He knew he might be a little burnt out from all of it, and he wasn't ready to commit to one side or the other just yet.

"I bet your dad can't wait for you to get back."

"Yeah," Michael said hesitantly. "He's been pushing for me to get out for a long time."

Sam sank back into his chair a bit more. "Well, my brothers have their own way of seeing the world. He probably just wants to have you around again. He's proud of you. We all are."

The room got quiet again when Michael didn't respond. Then Sam sighed and leaned forward. "I'm turning in, soldier. You have a good night." Sam hefted himself out of his chair, leaving Michael to turn off the TV and find his way to his own bed.

# CHAPTER 11

THE NEXT MORNING MICHAEL GOT UP, HAD ANOTHER shower, and ate an over-the-top breakfast prepared by his aunt. With their coffee and huevos rancheros in front of them, Sam asked Michael where he was off to next.

"Las Vegas, to see Uncle Patrick."

At the sound of the name Sam twitched. Patrick was Sam's twin, almost perfectly alike physically yet the exact opposite when it came to personality. Due to politics and ideology, they were no longer on speaking terms. Their social media exchanges were a back-and-forth of vitriol. Patrick was a liberal, a term used as an insult in this house. Sam turned his head, not looking at Michael. "Give my brother my best wishes."

They said their goodbyes and Michael was once again on the road. West Texas, from San Antonio to El Paso, was nothing but dirt and the occasional gas station. He was doing his best to get through it quickly. The route, the same he'd taken in reverse when he'd left California, didn't at all enliven his dull memories of the dry, desolate drive. His conversation with his uncle rattled in his mind, a nagging push toward choosing his side. The divisions between his two uncles, he couldn't help thinking, reflected something bigger.

He drove north of El Paso, heading toward the Texas border that jutted halfway into New Mexico. He had friends who were stationed out here and debated stopping in to see them. They didn't stray too far from the military post and avoided going over the Southern border completely. He thought about being with them, safe and paddocked behind the walls of Fort Bliss. Michael couldn't see himself driving onto another military post after leaving Fort Campbell. He kept driving until he was well outside the city limits.

He chose to sleep in his car instead, out at a rest stop, his the only vehicle. It was, perhaps, an unspoken challenge to the rest of the world, him camping out in this more vulnerable position, so near to the border. He reached down beneath the seat and put a reassuring hand on the Glock 19 stowed there. The dry mountain scenery out over the desert landscape of the Mesa calmed him, a familiar and strange comfort that let him sleep without the help of the bottle.

# CHAPTER 12

He had gone to bed early and, as such, had risen early, right before dawn. It was how he had done it for so many years. As he got out and stretched in the waking sun, he wondered if this discipline would hold now that he was no longer in the service.

The early start meant he got to his Uncle Patrick's house at a decent hour, soon finding himself wrapped in a hug.

"Welcome to Las Vegas!" Patrick boomed.

"Thanks!" While they embraced two German Shepherds encircled them both, feeding off the energy of the happy motion, trying to greet Michael in the same way. "You're looking good, Uncle Patrick, but I guess that's the benefit of nightlife in Sin City."

Patrick laughed and slapped him on the back, leading him into the house. "I think it does help. I know you're on your way home, kid, otherwise I'd take you out and show you how we really do it. For now, let's get you cleaned up. You smell like Texas."

"We're not hitting the town?"

"We could, kid, but I don't want to mess up my game by having my sweet baby nephew play wingman."

Once, when Michael was younger, back when the uncles still talked, Patrick had told him with a wink, "I love the Air Force because I get paid to bounce around the globe and sample its women." Retired now, he lived off his pension and his consultation work. Michael did think he looked younger than his twin. He still smoked and drank too much, but he did it with a carefree attitude that seemed to counterbalance the negative effects.

"Besides, kid, you and I got a lot to talk about." With that, he pushed closed the door and showed him around, letting him drop his things before underhanding him a beer from his fridge. "Here, this should get you started."

They soon loaded up in his truck and went closer to the strip to a very comfortable and expensive tavern that served exceptional steaks and stiff drinks. After catching up on the various aspects of each other's lives, the conversation shifted after Michael mentioned that Patrick's brother sent his best.

His uncle slid back in his chair a bit. "You know, that guy," he said, biting off the words, "he just doesn't get it." He took a long sip and leaned in. "The entire country, regardless of the war, is in decent shape. The economy, which the Republicans destroyed, is up. We're finally getting out of those fucking wars, making progress there. I'm sure you have mixed feelings about this, but you have to have seen how many good efforts were blocked by Congress, how much interference the Republicans caused. They cried wolf so many times about the unconstitutionality of the president and shut down the government several times, and for what? So that universal healthcare wouldn't get through? The Supreme Court said it's constitutional, it got through Congress. It's law. Get the fuck over it."

Michael looked into his glass, unsure how to respond, while Patrick launched into a tirade about all conservatives being racist. He didn't agree with everything his uncle was saying, but he didn't feel any love for anybody in Congress either. Having pay blocked several times while in Afghanistan so a bunch of overdressed people in air conditioning and comfortable chairs could debate budget tends to piss a soldier off. Michael traveled throughout the U.S. and lived in several different states, so he knew to expect this cultural change when entering different regions of the country. But his uncles seemed such strongly opposed forces on either side of him. "Uncle Patrick," Michael said, interrupting his tangent. "Don't you think, after working in government your whole life, that we tend to be stuck on certain things? I mean, you must have encountered as much bureaucratic bullshit as I've dealt with. I've seen the Fed fuck up enough to know that I don't want them in charge of too many aspects of my life."

Patrick looked annoyed. "With that attitude social progress doesn't occur. Gay marriage wouldn't have been legalized because who gives a shit about that?"

"I'm not saying that wasn't the right move. I'm only wondering if the federal government isn't too involved in dictating how things should be done."

"That's where you're wrong, kid. We're all Americans, and what goes for one part as far as law goes should work for everyone else." Patrick set his glass down in a stern manner that suggested his point was made. But when Michael looked up at his uncle he noticed a flirtatious smile on him as their male waiter approached. Maybe there was a reason he'd brought up gay marriage, but Michael did not want to press him on it and merely shrugged it off.

After a moment, Patrick returned to his former fun composure. "I bet your dad can't wait for you to get back."

Michael took a long drink of his beer. "Yup, he's been pushing for me to get out for a long time."

"I'm sure he'll be thrilled. Last time I talked to him he seemed to be in a great place. New wife is working out well for him, huh?"

"Yeah, he seems pretty happy." He shrugged. "To be honest I don't really know her, so I don't really know how things are going."

"Well, I think it's good for him." He paused, looking someplace behind Michael, then brought his attention back to him. "You're a registered democrat, right?"

Michael looked down and gave his head a shake, thinking about his conversation with Patrick's brother. "Uncle Patrick, politics are the last thing on my mind after what I've been through."

"I get it, but you understand more than most the consequences of political action. You're going back to California and you're going to have to reevaluate a lot. Politics one of them." He paused for a bit. "But get settled in first, I guess," he said, draining his beer. "Alright, bud, let's head home. I've got to feed my fur babies, and I've got a good bottle we can crack open."

They headed back and had a few more drinks while giving the dogs the attention they demanded. A couple of times Patrick tried steering the conversation back to politics, but Michael did his best to deflect and change the subject. The night ended with Michael in the guest bedroom sharing a twin bed with both the dogs.

# CHAPTER 13

THE EXCESS OF DRINKS LEFT MICHAEL SLEEPING IN LATER than he usually did. He woke to the bed empty of shepherds and his head groggy. He went to his uncle's kitchen, where a pot of coffee waited, a mug at the ready and a bottle of whiskey on standby. He poured himself a cup with a generous splash from the bottle. He then ventured into the living room and took a seat looking out the glass doors leading to the balcony. Sipping his coffee, he let the caffeine and alcohol bring him back to balance as he took in the desert mountains outside of Las Vegas. The view along with the drink eased him into the new day.

Michael was getting up for a refill when Patrick came in with the dogs. "Good morning! Leveled out yet?" he asked, releasing the shepherds from their leashes.

"Almost," Michael replied as he did his best to navigate through the circling dogs to enter the kitchen.

"Well, I'm sure you're eager to hit the road. How long has it been since you left for the army?" Patrick asked as he grabbed a water from the refrigerator.

"Ten years."

"That's all?" Patrick laughed. "I'm sure some things have changed, but there will be a lot that hasn't. The biggest change might just be you, Bud."

"Guess I'll find out."

"I bet your father has a hell of a homecoming set up for you."

Michael nodded and shrugged.

"Just keep your head down and go to school. You've got a solid plan, trooper. Stick to it. Everything else will fall into place." Patrick was now prepping the dog's food. "Sorry I don't have anything for breakfast. I only eat once a day. Probably should have picked something up for you while we were on our jog."

"No worries," Michael said, shrugging it off. "I'll pick something up on the road."

Patrick nodded as he gave the dogs their bowls. Michael returned to the living room to finish his coffee. Once he finished the cup he went back to the guest room, cleaned himself and the area, packed his bag, then said his farewells to the dogs and his uncle.

As he left Michael replayed both of the discussions with his uncles in his head. Both men were unable to concede their points or the arguments. You either agreed with them or you were wrong. It was clear to him that they were both trying to steer him into their way of thinking when they balked any time he talked moderation. To them, there was no middle ground. Bullheaded, the both of them.

The next leg of his journey felt more like a short sprint. Yet the closer he got to California, the more he ran through his uncles' words. That icy grip, albeit lessened, returned around his heart. Was it excitement? Anxiety? Dread? If so, why did that anger keep burning back up? That anger that pushed him to leave this area in the first place. Anger that, now that he'd returned, had no direction for release. How had it never been resolved? Where was it coming from?

Flickers of broken memories of family squabbles tormented him to the point that he had to actively stop himself from accidentally hitting other drivers. Was that what had angered him? Was that what drove him to leave in the first place? Or was his anger heightened due to a career in aggressiveness, everything broken now more infuriating?

It all peaked as he crossed the border into California and stayed with him as he continued the long drive, heading north on I-5. It took all his discipline to not reach into the back seat to find comfort with a bottle.

All of this, coming back now? Was it the anticipation of picking up where he had left off? Was it something more?

His nerves calmed as he got into more familiar territory, his emotions more clearly excitement as he turned west toward the San Luis Reservoir, an area where he had spent a lot of time hunting and fishing with his father. The better memories soared in—roaming the hills with his friends tracking deer, four-wheeling and the struggle of getting the vehicles out of the mud. He sank deep into these recollections, wondering if he could get back to having fun times like he'd had before he left. Maybe, though, Patrick was right. Maybe he'd changed too much for all that. Lost on this thought, it took him a while to realize that he had been driving past the reservoir for the past fifteen minutes.

It was empty.

Roughly an hour later he pulled into his father's two-acre ranch in San Benito County. His anxiety wound tight as he stepped down out of the truck and walked to the front door. The door was locked, the property empty, the atmosphere of no one having been here in days undeniable. He had messaged his father in the months and weeks leading up to his trip, telling him the exact day he was coming back. Had he forgotten? He went to the side door and found the spare key under the doormat, letting himself in. He explored the house. No note, no indication that anyone had been here in the last few days.

Michael couldn't ignore the icy grip any longer and began searching through cabinets, opening and closing their doors with a harsher and harsher hand. He knew he could solve this problem by going to his truck, but this was supposed to be his house too. This was supposed to be where what he needed, he found. A safe space where he would always be welcome. The search itself took on a meaning of its own. Scanning the refrigerator shelves row by row. Cursing at cups and plates, pots and pans. Toppling spices and a pile of potatoes. What started out as a calm and controlled search turned into a frenzy as he tore open the pantry doors. If he could just find it here, he'd belong here.

Finally, he opened the door that revealed what he was looking for. Ignoring the labels, he nabbed the closest bottle within reach. After a long pull, Michael relaxed, allowing his body to slide down next to the cabinet. Slowly his breathing returned to normal as his senses dulled. He hadn't noticed the panic happening, but his hand must have been twitching, because as the alcohol did its work, his shaking hand slowly stopped trembling, going from a fast twitch to a slow pulse that ticked in time with his wristwatch. He took another drink and watched as his hand stopped pulsing and went steady.

# PART THREE
# TERCIO DE VARAS

*"But in the end one needs more courage to live than to kill himself."*
—Albert Camus

# CHAPTER 14

"I'm sorry it's got to be this way, kiddo, but you got to go." Michael's father was walking him out of the house to his truck.

"You could have given me a bit more heads-up than this."

His father shook his head. "Maybe someday when you're married, you'll understand." He looked back toward the house. "I didn't want to tell you this, but you scare the missus, and besides"—he swung his hand around and clasped the back of Michaels neck, sending pain shooting throughout his spine and arms—"my liquor cabinet is looking a little lighter."

Michael gritted his teeth to not show the pain. "It's only been a few weeks. She doesn't even know me."

His father looked at him curiously. "You got anger issues, bud. We're all worried that you have PTSD. So you should look into getting help for that."

Michael opened his truck door and stood there for a moment looking to a place beyond the fields of the ranch house. Wanting to scream at his father for enticing him home only to kick him out. Feeling like a second-class citizen, a demoted footnote in his father's new family structure, something to be feared and pushed away. He couldn't get angry though. That would only feed into what his father was saying. "I'll figure it out," he said, and climbed into his truck.

"Atta boy. I'll see you soon." His father closed the door for him.

He drove off, doing his best to keep a straight face amid the pain and bitterness. A few streets away he pulled off to the side of the road and reached into the back seat. Michael lifted a bottle out and took several long gulps, then reached into the center console and found a bottle of Motrin 800 mg tablets that he had stashed there. He fished out one of the horse-pills, popped it into his mouth, and chased it down with another pull from the bottle. Then he sat back and took several deep breaths in and out, eyes closed. He opened his eyes. "Okay." He drove off.

Michael really didn't have any place else to go. While he searched for a place to live, he purchased a cheap inflatable mattress that he slept on in the bed of his truck, parking alongside the backcountry roads he knew from when he was a kid. It took a few weeks, but he finally found a place to stay out in the hills, close enough to town that he told himself he wasn't isolating, only removing himself enough from humanity to keep his mind at ease and allowing himself enough space to roam and stay somewhat active.

His military service didn't count much toward college credits, but how could the bookish academic advisor at the community college know the extent of what he had done? Unless it was already established in her computer by some government official, she had no real power to tally up the decade of experience Michael had earned. He was forced to humble himself and play the game. It was "yes ma'am" and "no ma'am" until finally she asked about his plans.

"You mentioned you're hoping to transfer to a four-year university. What was your end goal for your education again?

"I'm not sure, but I do want to stay in the medical field."

"Ah, I see," she said, frowning as her gaze fell on Michael's wristband. "I'll create a pre-med degree plan for you. This will cover all the prerequisites so you can transfer as a biology major and figure out what direction to take when you get accepted into a university."

"Excellent. When do I start?"

"You'll have to wait until next semester. In the meantime..." She turned to her computer, hit a button, and a printer roared to life. "I'm going to give you some local resources." She glanced at his wrist again. "In case you have any... difficulties or issues during the interim."

Michael took the paper, a list of contacts—the Veterans Affairs suicide hotline, the local VFW and American Legion, and Alcoholics Anonymous among them. He stared at the paper, then back at the woman, who ignored him while she created his schedule.

Maybe she'd caught a whiff of the sips he'd taken from his flask-sized bottle of Johnny Walker Black prior to coming to her office. More likely, he was simply a combat veteran she had prejudged before he had even sat down. Everything about him from his clothes to his haircut practically shouted veteran before his paperwork confirmed it.

Too much time between exiting service and his upcoming school semester left him exploring the darker recesses of his memory and imagination. Alcohol countered the more vivid manifestations. He took to keeping a permanent rotating bottle in his center console. Months went by, and a once proud body began to waste from lethargy and excess as he battled with the transition to an uncertain future.

Once the semester did start, he added a pack of spearmint gum to his center console and tried his best to melt into the back of the classrooms and avoid being called on. Avoid being seen. It couldn't be helped. There was no chance of him blending in with students a decade younger than him. Especially in these smaller community college classrooms, the teachers wanted to get to know you or insert you in some group activity. So Michael would have to announce some interesting fact about himself, which inevitably meant telling everyone he was a veteran. The professors all had varying ways of singling him out too; one congratulated him on surviving, another wouldn't stop thanking him for his service and looking at him with concerned eyes.

The students on campus acted no different. One of them pulled him to the side after class and asked if he was alright up here, pointing to his own skull. There was never a right answer to any of these interactions. When he was on campus, though, he was focused, which at least helped him brush off these awkward encounters where he was treated either as a hero or a leper. Michael wasn't here to make friends; he saw school as a job, a stepping stone to that magical place called success.

# CHAPTER 15

HE SETTLED INTO A ROUTINE, STARTED VENTURING OUT more. Being back in familiar territory meant revisiting old haunts, trying old phone numbers. He ran into Kent, a bull of a man he had gone to high school with and who worked in the trades. They met outside of a liquor store, both stocking up on their weekly supplies, and smoothed themselves into small talk.

"You still hunt?" Kent eventually asked.

"I would. Haven't been out for a long time."

"Well, shit. What are you doing this weekend? I've got a duck club on the other side of the valley and an open spot."

"Duck hunting? Don't really have any gear for that."

"Worry not, ya old war hero. I got everything you need, just come on out."

Michael ignored the war hero comment. "Sounds good. It'll be good to get out of town for a bit."

They headed out that Friday, loading up Kent's truck with shotguns, ammo, waders, and extra warm clothing for the early morning chills they'd face. Kent had two giant coolers in the back of the truck, both filled to the brim, courtesy of his and Michael's liquor runs. "Think we'll have enough to survive the weekend?" Kent asked, smirking.

Michael laughed. "Might be rolling a bit light."

"Don't worry, there's enough to have a few breakfast beers in the blind to steady your hand before the ducks start flying."

"What about food?" Michael asked, noticing there wasn't anything other than liquids in the truck.

"Don't worry about that either. We'll have a feast prepared for us every night."

They closed the tailgate and got on the road, bumping over the pass that Michael had come over a few months ago.

It was a moonless night when they entered the marshlands. The duck club was more of a bright shanty town of trailers that contrasted the night like a casino beckoning them in. The only permanent cover was an overhang that stemmed from a bathroom and an outdoor sink, a cleaning station for their birds. A giant BBQ smoked with meat and an assortment of foods were laid out on the picnic tables under the overhang. Half a dozen men stood around the BBQ pit critiquing the attendant, drinks in hand. Dogs bounced around the camp happily, chasing each other or the rabbits brave enough to come within sight.

Kent made the introductions, only one of them a familiar face. Louie was another bruiser in the trades Michael knew from years ago. He was a few years older with a giant beard.

At his side was a dog almost identical to him, a giant chocolate lab built like a pit bull. "Michael, I haven't seen you in a coon's age!" he said, and wrapped him in a giant bear hug. "Let's get drunk so you can tell me about the war."

"As long as you don't try snapping my spine again!" Michael said, and Louie let him down.

"America treating you good?"

"It's getting there. It's good to be home. This your dog?" Michael asked as the brutish animal waddled over and leaned all his weight against his legs, almost toppling him.

"Yup. Raised him from a pup. This here is Trigger," Louie said as he poured a stream of beer out near the head of the dog, who greedily lapped it up out of the air. Between the scratches and beer, he was clearly in heaven.

"How is he in the blind?" Michael asked.

"Oh, he's a pain in the ass, but he'll fetch 'em up. The big moose whines nonstop between the action."

Kent tossed a piece of meat to the dog. "The four of us got a 4 am wake-up," he said with a nod to the dog, "so we better start drinking heavily now." With that, he produced a bottle of tequila and passed it to Michael. "Catch up to Trigger, there."

"If I must." Michael accepted the bottle and took a slow, satisfying swig.

In the morning, they roused their heavy heads and got dressed, fitting themselves into waders and packing extra shotgun shells and beers in their blind bags. They stepped out into the freezing pre-dawn air. Someone in the camp had brewed coffee; the men added decent pours of whiskey to clear their heads. Leveled off by the booze and energized by the caffeine, they gathered their gear and went off into the marshes, Trigger splashing contentedly about them as they waded through waist-high water.

The blind was on a small island where the tule reeds had been cut down to open up visibility from the wooden structure that stood six feet away from the water. Chairs waited for them with a spot for the dog to lie down as it waited for the guys to shoot down a bird. They made themselves as comfortable as they could get in the cold, then waded out to arrange decoy ducks in a rough J-hook. They still had about thirty minutes before they could legally start shooting. In the lull, they cracked open their first beers.

"Nothing like an all-American morning, aye Michael?" Kent asked after his first gulp.

"Better than an Afghanistan morning," Michael said as he sipped his.

"I'll bet," Louie said as he got Trigger to lie down. "You still remember how to use that thing?" He gestured at Michael's borrowed shotgun.

"We'll find out."

They had a relatively successful hunt, even after shooting more than hitting as they laughed, drank, and occasionally yelled at the dog for going the wrong direction for a downed bird. Michael managed to get three birds, while Kent and Louie each managed to take down six. A few hours later the sky grew calm and empty. Their packs empty too, not a beer to be had, they decided to head back.

They did their best to clean the birds of their feathers, finding some difficulty with Trigger stealing a bird every chance he got. After they got the meat processed and packed away, Louie slapped Michael on the back. "Glad you made it out. Soon enough, you'll be knocking them out of the sky."

Michael looked at the duck meat he had gotten, enough to have a few meals this week that weren't take-out or fast food, and felt proud. "I'm glad too. It's something to be out here, kicking it with the boys." He knew, at least, it was better than sitting in his cabin by himself. He bent down as Trigger waddled over to him and lay down at his feet for belly rubs. "This is a hell of a dog."

"He's a good gun dog. Not the brightest, but he gets the job done."

"Always loved dogs. We had a few dog handlers on deployment—you know, for sniffing out explosives and stuff. I think they were German Shepherds or Belgian Malinois. One time we were doing battle drills and the handlers had them off leash. The dogs got a kick out of jumping over us while we simulated a firefight."

Louie bent down to pet Trigger. "Bet they thought y'all were playing."

"Yeah." Michael's eyes went to the horizon. "I was friends with one of the handlers and he let me play with his dog, Crumb. We used to argue about who was going to adopt him after the army retired him."

"So I take it he got the dog?"

Michael looked down at Trigger, who was on his back, happily getting his belly rubbed down by Louie. The dog's eyes rolled into the back of his head. Trigger licked his lips a few times, near to falling asleep under the rhythm of the massage. Michael wondered if he himself had ever been as content with life as this dog was in this moment. "No, the dog got hit."

# CHAPTER 16

THE HUNT PROMPTED MICHAEL TO END HIS SELF-isolation, improving his outlook on a potential life outside the army. Being older than the students around him and not wanting to mix work with pleasure, he turned to dating apps to find more social engagement. He got a lot of matches only to have conversation drift off into failed human connection in the digital world. Finally, he matched with someone who sent his mind to fantasy, and after a few days of conversing online, they met at a coffee shop.

Evelyn was small with a petite frame. Brunette hair framed an immaculate smile. Her olive skin and almond-shaped brown eyes hinted at some genetic connection to the other side of the Pacific in addition to her clearly Caucasian roots. Her photos did her no justice at all.

They ordered their coffees and found a comfortable spot in the cozy cafe. At first, easy links between their different hobbies, interests, and ambitions had conversation flowing easily. Then Michael saw her eyes change and knew the conversation was going to shift.

"So you just got out of the army?"

He took a hesitant sip from his cup. "Yeah, I've been out for a few months now."

"How long did you serve?"

"Ten years."

"Wow. And did you have to go over there at all?" She gestured over her shoulder.

Nodding. "Yeah, I did two tours to Afghanistan."

"That must have been intense. How was it?"

Michael, looking out the window and off toward the rolling green hills, set his coffee on the short table between them. "It's a beautiful country. Giant mountains, deep valleys. It's kind of like stepping back in time. Especially with how the tribal Afghans live. Of course, the downside is they're trying to kill you," he added with an awkward chuckle.

She didn't chuckle back; her eyes seemed to water a bit.

Michael couldn't read the expression on her face, so he looked back out the window. "It was an experience, but it's done with. How's your coffee?"

She looked down at her cup. "It's good."

A couple of seconds passed as Michael searched for something neutral to bring up; he couldn't let it end in this awkward moment. "So you're going to school too, right? Where at?"

She lifted her face and perked up a bit. "I'm up at state."

"Cool, what are you studying?"

A smile returned to her face. "I'm majoring in communications."

# CHAPTER 17

THE NEXT FEW DAYS WERE BLISS FOR MICHAEL. TEXTING, flirting, and a second date ending with a passionate kiss. Emotions he had buried for years flickered back to life and he imagined that he was getting somewhere close to happiness. He was feeling alive, all the colors of the world vibrant, all those dark and intrusive thoughts gone—or at least pushed aside. The bottles in his hillside cottage and the one in his truck kept their levels as his soul shed some of its burden. He still couldn't quite shake the feeling that something wasn't right about where he was at when he was alone and in his own head, but at least when he was engaged with Evelyn, his mind wasn't confused. Maybe she was what he needed.

They had their third date at Evelyn's apartment for dinner and a movie. He was nervous and excited. It had been a long time since he'd been with a woman. Not since before this last tour, and that had been financially arranged; he hadn't wanted to connect with anyone that way until he was sure he was settled. Settled with himself or in a location, he couldn't say.

He resisted the urge to take a pull from the bottle in his center console as he parked at her apartment complex, wanting something to take the edge off but also not wanting to go in smelling like whiskey. Instead, he grabbed the wine bottle from the passenger seat and stepped up to her apartment door.

She answered his knocks, opening the door to a small all-white apartment. Evelyn, dressed in black leggings and a matching tank top, embraced him and they kissed. "Come on in," she said, taking his hand and leading him inside. "I'm not much of a cook, so I thought we could order a pizza."

"That'll pair well with the wine."

She laughed and took the bottle from him, setting it on the faux marble countertop. "So sophisticated."

Michael shrugged and kicked off his boots near the doorway. "I try."

"Make yourself at home. Why don't you pick out a movie while I order. Any toppings you like, don't like?"

"I'm a carnivore, but there's nothing I can't throw down, so order what you like," he said as he walked into the carpeted living area. He took a seat on the heavily cushioned sofa that faced a decent-sized flat-screen television, picked up a remote control from the glass coffee table in front of the couch, and browsed for a film.

A few moments later Evelyn joined him with a pair of wine glasses that she set on the coffee table, ensuring a coaster sat under each of them. Michael leaned over, lifted his glass, and took a healthy drink of it. Evelyn got close to him as they debated on the options he'd found, both settling on what looked like a mediocre romantic comedy that Michael hoped they wouldn't get a chance to finish.

The food arrived and they moved from the couch to the kitchen, where Evelyn had set out plates and napkins. They ate, drank, and exchanged small talk between bites. They finished the pizza and refilled their wine glasses, moving back to the couch to resume the movie. About forty-five minutes in, Michael made his move, leaning in to give Evelyn a kiss. She responded by further leaning her body into his. She moved her hand to his inner thigh and their passion grew. Slowly withdrawing from his lips, she stood up and took his hand, leading him into her bedroom.

The bedroom was as white as the living room, lit only by strings of clear Christmas lights draped above the bed. As she led him in, she turned around, kissing him again, wrapping herself around him, pulling him down onto the bed. Their clothes scattered across the floor and she put protection on Michael. Then they brought themselves together, letting passion overtake them both and growing heated in their throes. Michael felt her convulse under him, keeping his rhythm as he let her have her moment. As he continued, he thought she was losing interest, and then he lost the connection.

Even as he fought to remain focused, Michael was losing his rigidity.

She looked up at him, panting. "What's wrong?"

"I'm sorry, it's—it's been a long time for me."

"You sure nothing's wrong?"

"Nothing's wrong. I just need a minute."

She scooted out from under him and propped herself up on the pillows. "Was it the wine?"

"No, I don't think it was the wine"

"Is it me?"

"No, it's definitely not you. I'm not sure what's going on."

She sighed and looked at him. "Well, nobody else I've been with has had this problem. Do you need some water or something?"

"No, thanks. I don't think that's it."

They sat there awkwardly for a few minutes while Michael tried to get his body to respond. In his head he cursed himself. This shouldn't be a problem. Looking at her face, he could see the disappointment, which only worsened things for him. The more he looked at her, the more he felt that this was such a stupid problem to have. Evelyn broke the silence.

"Well, I've got an early morning tomorrow, and I sleep better alone."

"Okay, sure." Michael got up off the bed and started putting his clothes on as she donned a pair of matching pajamas. "I'll see you soon, right?"

She flipped her hair out of the neck of the silk top. "I have plans this weekend, but let's see how next week turns out. Okay?"

"Okay," he said as she led him to the door, and leaned down to give her a kiss. "Have a good night."

"Good night, Michael." With that, she closed the door behind him.

# CHAPTER 18

When Kent called him up for another weekend out duck hunting, he didn't hesitate. Michael knew that he was too inside his own head to hang around with his own thoughts after the other night. Kent picked up Michael the next day, and they went through the ritual of stockpiling enough booze to open their own bar. Truck loaded, they drove through the hill pass into the central valley, once again arriving after dark with a waxing moon sneering down on them, dark clouds looming over the hills behind them.

"Looks like we're in front of a storm," Michael said as he got out of the truck.

Kent looked back at the incoming clouds. "Yup. Should kick some things up, maybe make for an interesting hunt? Don't know, ask Louie. It's been raining really heavy over here for the past week."

Michael nodded and trekked into the center of the club, greeted first by Trigger, wagging his whole body with excitement as he approached. Louie was right behind him with a beer can in each hand. "Welcome back! Looks like Trigger sure missed you."

"Good to be back." Michael bent down and gave the animal its due love. "How do you think tomorrow is going to work out with the weather moving in?"

Louie handed Michael one of the beers. "It's going to be rough; I don't think we'll have a good spot." He looked over at the dark masses moving over the hills toward them. "It's going to storm all night for sure. We've needed the rain for a long time, but last week's downpours practically flooded the fields out here. The ducks loved it, but we'll see if we get a spot where they'll actually land and stay. You doing alright?"

Kent walked up with a bottle of tequila. "Yeah, how's that liberal education you're getting on my tax dollar going?"

Michael grunted. "Started seeing this cute little honey." His voice came out more confident than he felt.

Kent handed the bottle to Michael. "Nice. What's her name?"

"Evelyn. Met her online."

"You got a picture?" Kent asked.

"Yeah." Michael dug out his phone and showed the guys her profile.

"I know her," Kent said with a glance at Louie.

"Yeah," Louie said. "Be careful with that one. She has a reputation for having a good time."

"What do you mean?"

"She's a partier. Meets up after swiping right a lot. Hops right back on those apps after first dates. Showed up in my feed

once and didn't get anywhere, but I recognized her downtown last weekend, out with a few other girls. She was flirting
with some guy. Not sure, but she might have left with him.
How long have you been seeing her?"

"Not long," Michael admitted.

Kent passed the bottle back to Michael. "Don't settle down
with the first floozy you meet now that you're back. Enjoy
yourself. Hell! You've earned it!"

Sighing, Michael took the bottle and allowed himself a long
pull. "Yeah, we'll see what happens." He tried pushing it to
the back of his mind, but he couldn't help his disappointment. A part of him cursed himself for even bringing her up,
like if he would have kept it to himself, this insecurity
wouldn't be there. That sense he might be on the right track
swerved back toward the letdown of hook-up culture.

They ate, continued to drink, Michael using the booze to
numb his thoughts. They finally went to one of the trailers as
the rain came pounding down. Unfazed by the cold and
approaching dawn, they drank and joked into the morning.
Their wake-up came quick, the storm still hitting hard. As
they dressed, Kent and Louie both commented that they
weren't going to have a good hunt with the weather and the
blind they were going to get this morning. Michael listened to
their complaints as he spiked his coffee. They packed a
couple of beers each as they took off in the darkness with
Trigger, planning to cut the day short if their expectation held
true.

No luck at the blind. The weather wasn't cooperating and the
ducks they did shoot at didn't seem to want to come down.
After several hours, the sky let up, but with no wind or rain

or ducks in sight, they decided to call it and head back to the club.

"You know, there might be a few wounded ducks on the aqueduct," Kent said as they waded back.

Louie looked at Trigger. "Could be we get something so we don't leave empty-handed."

"I'm down," Michael said as they tromped through the marshes to the aqueduct, which was on the other side of the road across from the duck club. Trigger loping alongside them, they walked along the rim. The water was high and flowing fast in the aqueduct, the drought that had left the reservoir dry when he first came back to California in the process of reversing under the heavy rains.

"I don't think I want to send Trigger into that," Louie said, looking at the rushing water.

"Yeah, not a good idea," Michael said, studying the current.

Kent looked at them. "Well, hell. Looks like today's a bust, boys."

The group turned for the club, Kent leading with Louie and Trigger at the rear. Michael had eyes on the club, a strange nostalgia swelling at the sight of the trailer rooftops and makeshift buildings. He was lost in the memories of some mountain outpost when Louie screamed.

*"TRIGGER, NO!"*

Michael, snapping his head to look over his shoulder, caught a glimpse of the tail end of the dog as he dove into the aqueduct, a duck frantically swimming away toward the other side.

Trigger swam determinedly after the fowl. The size and strength of the dog seemed to be letting it contend with the current. As he watched from the earthen embankment on top of the slopped concrete canal, it seemed that Trigger might actually reach its target. Louie, though, was still screaming for Trigger to come back. That's when Michael saw that the water rushing through the wide concrete canal funneled toward an outlet pipe hidden somewhere beneath the surface. Trigger, in a deep focus on the duck, remained unaware that the current was pulling him faster than he could pursue his target. Michael joined Louie in yelling, neck aching as he bent it so as not to lose sight of the dog.

The dog, picking up the panic in their voices, finally turned around. They saw the frantic look as the dog tried to paddle toward them, eyes wide, body in a frenzy. Trigger's chest rose out of the water; the effort failed, and he fell backward into the watery vortex, disappearing.

Louie ran in a panic to the other side. Kent and Michael spread themselves out, but not before Michael heard Kent utter, "We're going to be pulling a dead dog out of that water."

Michael tried to keep track of time. Five minutes passed. Kent left to get rope while Louie screamed for his dog. Ten minutes passed. Still nothing.

Trigger's body finally bobbed up. Louie rushed down into the water with a rope attached to him, Kent and Michael holding on to the other end. Careful not to get sucked into the current, Louie wrapped an arm around the lifeless body of the dog, and Kent and Michael on the bank hauled them both out. Together they got Trigger's body out of the embankment and up onto flat ground. They were all silent, sobered by the moment. Louie, as soaked as the animal, stroked the wet pelt, eyes red.

Michael could do nothing but stare. A memory crept into his brain. Another dog a lifetime ago, in some dusty corner of Afghanistan, tearing his heart apart.

# CHAPTER 19

They cut the weekend short, Louie heading back to his house, Michael and Kent to theirs. The whole ride back, the base of Michael's neck flared angrily, pain soaring down both arms.

Back in his cabin, he slept uneasily but for a long time, waking up a half dozen times drenched in sweat—so much so that he had to keep a towel next to the bed to dry himself off, only to crawl back into soaked sheets. Michael wasn't sure, but he thought he could hear the echo of his own scream as he woke once. Another time, he came to but couldn't move, struggling to the point of panic as he tried to convince his body to obey his commands until he found control, gasping for breath. He sat awake for hours in between, frustrated he had no control over these things. That he couldn't push these emotions back down. He eventually ended up staring at a bottle, angry at himself for feeling the need to drink, then took a pull from it and finally got back to sleep.

The week started and he went back to school, very conscious of the fact that Evelyn hadn't messaged him. Every second that ticked away without contact fueled his jealousy. He tried to fight the negativity and sent a text one evening to see if she wanted to get dinner that week. It took a day for her to reply that this week was no good. The response stung. He tried telling himself that it was no big deal, that it was too soon to read too much into anything. Buried the emotions with a drink. Another after that when the first didn't work. Tried to regain control.

*Call her, tell her what you think about her blowing you off, about what you heard this weekend.*

The invasive thought repeated. The frustration turned into anger. He went from staring at his phone to staring at the wall. Michael pulled up her contact information, thumb hovering over the call button, only to back out of it. Over and over, he looked at her phone number. Then in a flash the number started dialing.

"Hello, Michael." She had picked up after what Michael imagined to be five minutes of ringing.

"Hey, so what's the deal here?"

"What are you talking about? Not getting dinner? I'm just tired. I've had a long week and want some time to myself."

*She's blowing me off.* "Really? Because I've had a rough week as well."

"I'm sorry to hear that, but I really would like to be alone this week."

"That's not what I heard," Michael blurted.

"What's that supposed to mean?"

"Well, I heard that you were out last weekend with another

guy, and now you don't want to hang out with me. How do you think that makes me feel?"

"Look, we haven't put a label on anything, so it's none of your business what I do when you're not around."

"We haven't put a label on anything? What the fuck are you talking about?"

Anger entered her voice. "What the fuck are *you* talking about? We went on a few dates, it was fun, that's it. I'm really not in the mood for whatever tantrum you're throwing right now. I'm going to hang up."

Michael pulled back on his own anger. "I'm sorry, but I've had an incredibly shitty weekend and I don't want to play this game. I just watched my buddy's dog die, and that's brought up some issues for me."

"So what? It's not like it was your dog. That's no reason to take it out on me."

The hand holding his phone went tight. "Look, my last girl-friend broke up with me while I was deployed. When I got back, I found out she was engaged and pregnant. So yeah, I got trust issues."

There was hesitation on Evelyn's side of the phone. The seconds ticked away. Then came an exacerbated nasal exhale. "Well, my fiancé cheated on me on Valentine's Day. You're not the only one who's been fucked over." The line went dead after that statement.

Michael looked at the phone incomprehensibly. Fifteen minutes ago, he was sure he was in the right. Now he wasn't certain at all. Was she lying? Was it the truth? Was he too fucked up in the head to comprehend any of it? Maybe he was crazy. Was it because he couldn't perform?

He threw the phone against the wall, screaming. Helpless. Helpless when *he* was the help. The one who everyone called upon to save them. Why couldn't he help himself?

He paced around the room, grabbed a bottle, tipped it to his lips. He moved to his bed and sat down heavily. He wanted to cry but he couldn't remember how. Instead he leaned into rage and frustration. Cursing God and women for this torment. Hating everyone—those who stayed behind, those who didn't choose to go at all and do what he did, those who said they loved him, those who passed away. The empty promise of a brighter future in contrast to a bleak past. He couldn't escape any of it. This was his life. This was all he would ever know. Frustration. Heartbreak. Where was all the glory he was promised for his time in service? Was this the life he had fought and sacrificed so much for? Death and people he couldn't trust?

In a blink, his hand shot to the dresser and opened the drawer. He pulled out the black 9mm pistol that sat in there and racked a round into the chamber. His fingers slid across the coarse grip of the handle, the blocky structure of the top of the slide over the barrel. He cradled the gun in his lap like a memento from a lost lover, enjoying its weight in his hands. All those books and movies celebrating the glory of battle wasted on the return home. He understood that deeply.

Slowly, deliberately, he gripped the handle with his right hand. Pulled the weapon up toward his head. Pressed the barrel to his temple. "This is it, fuck it." He moved his finger to the trigger and put pressure on it.

He exhaled and took the gun away from his temple, leaving a pale circular imprint after the blood flow there cut off with the barrel's pressure.

He'd been holding his breath. Started hyperventilating. He brought the gun back down into his lap, looking at it now resting in his palms. At the hardened plastic of the grip, at the metal of the barrel, at the grooves near the hammer, so easily allowing the slide to pull back to chamber a bullet. He consciously noted its every detail, allowing his breathing to return to normal. Then he hit the magazine release, letting it fall into his opposite hand, and set it on the dresser. He grabbed the slide back and allowed the bullet to fly out, catching it in midair. He set it down next to the magazine. Putting the pistol on the table, he sat and stared at the lone bullet sitting upright on the dresser.

Lost and alone, he thought about all of his friends still in the army. Wishing he was back in Afghanistan where life made sense. Where he didn't have to navigate his emotions or those of other people. There, he had felt powerful, in control. There, he was the master of his fate. Here, he seemed out of place, disconnected. He thought about all the conversations with his friends outside of the military, how every one of them agitated him on some level. Michael thought also of Trigger, wondering why the dog's end hurt him more than anything else. Maybe it was the death of something innocent, a reflection of himself from deep in his past. Was he allowing himself to be goaded and moved, or was this fate? Was there a difference?

He sat like that alone with his thoughts and his gun until the sun came up, eventually realizing there was nothing left for him to do but get up and move on.

## Chapter Twenty

. . .

It took him several months to settle down and recover, the pain in his neck receding. He managed his urges the same way he did in Afghanistan, alone with a collection of material that was shared from peer to peer. He binge-watched the smut, hating the fact that he was watching the crap, hating how grotesque and graphic it became, how he was viewing things beyond anything he'd ever do with another person. After each viewing and self-pleasuring episode, he'd sit in a state of self-disgust, vaguely wondering how to regain his composure.

He ventured out only for food and class. The one time he did deviate, he went back to the coffee shop where he met Evelyn. He imagined it was his subconscious or maybe his curse leading him back there. As he waited in line, he noticed her there, as if a mirage, another guy sitting across from her. He quickly paid for his coffee and left. Jumping into his truck, he saw her exiting the coffee shop with him. He caught her eye. The brief look he got, her face said one thing: Fear.

He drove away.

Was that the image that he constantly presented now that he was back in the civilian world? Had his personality changed so much that he was now a constant projection of what he knew himself capable of? One thing he knew for sure, he didn't want to have stalker attached to his name. He decided he'd avoid Evelyn at all costs.

Letting his loneliness guide him, he turned another corner of the internet to explore options. He browsed picture and profiles, checking for reviews until comfortable with his choice, and set up an appointment for the next day after class. She gave him a general direction for where to go, then about five minutes before their set time, she gave him an address. Once he texted that he'd parked, he was given an apartment number.

As he knocked on the door, his heart raced. He was still scanning the parking lot as the door opened to reveal a darkened room, an obscured feminine figure gesturing him in.

"Welcome. Come in."

Slipping in through the slightly open door, he managed a quick glance to confirm it was the person he was there to see and, stepping in further, kept his eyes moving to make sure they were alone. After closing the door behind him, she turned to Michael, embracing him with a kiss on the cheek. "Hi. I'm Lilith."

Michael took her in. She was red-headed, with porcelain skin and green eyes, wearing nylon stockings and, with no shoes, only a few inches shorter than him. Her plaid miniskirt met a bare midriff. A white tight tank top exposed unnaturally perky cleavage held up by a purple brassiere. Her face was heavily made up, and her demeanor had a professional calm to it.

She sensed his tension and, with a slight smirk, guided him deeper into the studio apartment. "Would you like a drink?"

"A drink would be perfect."

"How does bourbon sound?"

"Still perfect."

She led him to the couch so he could sit down. Michael studied her figure as she walked away toward the kitchen island. He took in the room, settling into a tentative ease. He heard her pour the drinks and turned to watch. In the short time that he had taken his eyes off her, she had lost the skirt and tank top. She sauntered over to him in beautifully laced purple lingerie, his female fantasy coming forth with his medicine. All worries left him as she sat down beside him and threw a stocking leg over his. "Cheers." They clinked their glasses together and downed the healthy pours.

The tension at the base of his neck unwound and shook loose as the bourbon took effect.

"Better?" she asked as she put her glass down on the coffee table in front of them.

"Much," he said, setting his tumbler down next to hers. Then he took the cash out of a pocket and set that down in between the two cups.

"Good. Why don't you go take a shower and come see me when you're dried off."

Michael did as he was told.

Thirty minutes later, he was lying with her in the crook of his arm, her head on his shoulder, both letting the other's sweat soak into the lingerie pieces she still wore. "Don't worry about it. It's more common than you think."

"It's just frustrating is all."

"You're in your head too much. Do you see me complaining about your performance?" She turned his head so he could see the satisfied grin on her face, then planted a kiss on his lips.

"Good to know that's not an issue."

Laughing, she rolled over to reach the nightstand, producing a pack of menthol cigarettes and a lighter. "That's definitely not your problem," she said, lighting one and taking a long drag.

Delicately, Michael took the cigarette from between her rouged lips and inhaled a dose of the smoke. "Well, it's still an issue for me," he said as he put it back.

She looked at him and frowned a bit, then rolled over to grab an ashtray from atop the nightstand. She got comfortable back in his embrace and balanced the ashtray between their bodies, sculpting the end of the cigarette into a point. As she did, her hand brushed against the bracelet on his wrist. "Have you tried getting help?"

"For what?"

She smirked. "Babe, you might have some issues. Call it a woman's intuition." She put the cigarette in the ashtray and then got up off the bed. As she did, Michael noticed a lily tattoo on her shoulder. He admired her figure as she walked away from him and went into the bathroom.

Michael leaned back and stared at the ceiling for a bit, thinking to himself. He could go to the VA, but he already knew what they'd do. The doctor would listen to his issues, nodding along, ticking off symptoms in his head, listening for those key words as he decided what antidepressant he'd prescribe. "No, thanks. This right here is far better therapy."

She giggled from the bathroom. "That may be true, but I'm expensive."

"As you should be," he said, and stole the cigarette from the ashtray for another drag. "And you get what you pay for." He returned the cigarette. "You could always take me on as a charity case. Pro bono. Could be a tax write-off for you."

She came back to the bed and snorted, stifling her laughter as she picked up the cigarette and took a drag. "Sorry, but I've got expensive tastes." Lilith blew smoke out. "Besides, grad school isn't cheap."

"What are you studying?"

She paused; Michael knew he had probed into something that she was keeping separate from what she was doing with him. He waited for her to respond, seeing that she had let something personal slip and needed a moment. "Psychology."

Michael nodding knowingly. "I guess that makes sense."

"I don't tell clients that. I don't want to face any judgment about the morality of what I do. Unless they've lived on the edges of society, seen some extremes, they don't really have a voice in opinion." She shrugged. "But I feel safe with you."

"Well, I think we're similar creatures," he said as he stroked her arm, causing her to lean into him more. "We both sacrificed and sold our innocence to try and get by in this world, or maybe just to get away from something. I agree with you on everyone else casting judgment. Fuck 'em."

Her fingertips danced along his abdomen, causing Michael's body to respond appropriately. "Maybe," she said; then, seeing the effect she had, added, "but let's forget that and take care of you."

"Round two?"

She tilted her head up, kissing him. "Mmmm. Have at it, soldier."

With that, they let their bodies fully entwine.

An hour later, Michael headed back to his truck having showered once more. Invigorated, he looked up and caught sight of the moon, full and glowing lovingly down on him. All pain and worries drained away from him.

He scanned the parking lot and climbed into the driver's seat. Inside, door closed, he opened the glove compartment, taking out his wallet and letting his hand glide over the pistol right next to it. After rechecking his surroundings, he took out the pistol. He dropped the magazine and unchambered the round that he had placed in the barrel before going up to her apartment. He returned the bullet to the magazine, put that back into the gun, and placed the pistol back in its spot in the glove box.

Taking a breath, he relaxed. Then, looking at his phone, he saw one new message. It was from First Sergeant Porter. Saying I've got some bad news, call me.

Not wanting to ruin his high, he hesitated. With a heavy sigh, Michael called his old boss.

After a few rings. "Hey, Doc, how ya been?"

"I'm alright, boss, what's going on?"

Porter paused on the other end. "So. It's about Conchord, he's dead."

"What?! How the fuck did that happen?"

Another hesitation. "I don't have the full details—we might not ever get the full details—but it looks like he got into a highway chase with the sheriff's department. We're not sure what happened precisely, but he ended up getting gunned down. I can send you more info when I have it."

Michael had slumped down in his seat as he heard the news. He didn't say anything, unable to push words out over the guilt rising in his chest.

"Hey! I know ya, Bubba. Don't start blaming yourself on this shit, okay? He could have called any one of us, and you know more than anybody else how his mind hasn't been the same since that blast. You good?"

Clearing his throat. "Yeah, I'm good."

"Just take it easy. Go grab a drink, get your head right."

Michael stared at the glove box for a long moment. Porter could have been calling Conchord with similar news not too long ago.

"When's the funeral?"

# PART FOUR
# TERCIO DE BANDERILLAS

*"Usually when people are sad, they don't do anything. They just cry over their condition. But when they get angry, they bring about a change."*
—Malcom X

# CHAPTER 20

It took two weeks for the funeral arrangements to be finalized because of the criminal investigation into Conchord's death. Bit by bit Michael got the full story. Conchord was on leave, staying at his home in Tennessee, when apparently, he "lost it." He called the sheriff's dispatch, telling the operator that he was armed and that, unless they sent someone to stop him, he was going to kill someone. He strapped on his body armor, grabbed a pistol, and jumped into his Dodge Charger, leading the cops on an hour-long chase until he eventually pulled over. In the ensuing standoff with the sheriff's deputies, he made what seemed like a move to the gun tucked in his waistband and about six of the deputies unloaded theirs into his body. The criminal investigation began to determine if the shooting was justified.

Michael forced himself to watch the leaked dashcam footage online. He saw Conchord's movement, perhaps too quick, toward his waist. The rest of his body, however, screamed that he didn't pose a threat. Michael trained with Conchord enough to know his stance when readying to shoot, his shoulders up and back like a fresh boxer's, not slumped as though one defeated. After the third time replaying it, Michael vowed never to watch it again.

He flew out for his funeral, and Porter picked him up. Despite the grim circumstances, they still found themselves excited by their reunion.

"Welcome back to the land of the free, you hippie. You need a haircut!" Porter shouted as Michael hopped up into his obscenely large truck.

"Thanks, dickhead. Although, you might be right. It might have been a mistake moving back to California."

"Ya think? Give it a few more years and you'll be dropping acid and eating magic mushrooms with the rest of them, gathered in a drum circle and meditating with crystals."

"That's not going to happen—I can't even smoke pot. I get too paranoid."

"Stick to God's nectar, that's what I always say. Here." Porter produced a bottle from his center console, the familiarity chilling. "This will help put your mind at ease."

"Thank you very much." Michael took a long drink and passed it back to Porter. "So I hear your wife's pregnant?"

"Yeah." Porter smirked. "Kind of sucks she got pregnant as soon as we started trying."

"You were trying to draw out her baby fever for more sex, you ape."

"Fuck yeah, Bubba. Only good thing about her being preg-nant already is she's willing to give me a blow job again."

Michael laughed. "She had that Jedi mind control over your Johnson, didn't she?"

Porter laughed. "Bub, she treated my junk like it was the fountain of youth."

"I mean, if you think about it, she's not technically wrong."

"I'm serious! She'd practically count how many times I'd shake it after a piss to make sure I wasn't wasting anything."

"She like those BRBs?"

"Haven't really gotten those after getting back from Afghanistan, but if I ever did get hard on the road like that, I'd get a text demanding I return home." Porter's smile went from ear to ear. "Why do you think I married this woman?"

"I don't know, the usual reasons. Better pay with dependents, more basic allowance for housing, tax write-offs."

"Nah, that was wife number one and two."

They both laughed at that and passed the bottle for another round.

A quiet fell between them as they merged onto the highway. The road seemed to go straight through to the horizon, the trees and electrical lines along the road on repeat. The only change in the scenery was the cars they passed and those that came at them from the opposite direction.

"Shitty thing about Conchord, eh Doc?" Porter said, breaking the silence.

"Yeah, I'm still processing it."

"I've already said it, but I'll say it again. Don't blame yourself. We both know he wasn't the same after that last concussion. That blast probably had a bigger effect than we could possibly imagine on his personality. Don't act like you don't remember the times the lights would turn off when you talked to him. There was nothing you or I could have done to stop what he got himself into. All of that is on him. He had a responsibility to take care of himself, just like you have a responsibility to take care of yourself. I'm sure it's weighing on you, but remember: Not. Your. Fault."

"We can both say that, but it's just that. I earned my combat medic badge treating him; in that gun fight I proved that I've got what it takes to be a war fighter and a medic. It feels like —I don't know—like that's lost its value somehow."

"That's that bullshit I was afraid of. Look, Bub, you did what you did and you were a hell of a soldier. No one can take that away from you. We don't control what our brothers do either while they're in or when they get out. We also don't control the outcome of the war; we just fight the battles in front of us. Look what happened in Iraq. Same thing could happen in Afghanistan. Not a damn thing we can do about it other than move on and take care of what's in front of us." He paused, then continued in a fatherly tone, "You should be proud of yourself. What did I always tell you? An infantryman cares only about three things: a good exit plan, a good medic, and good food. With you around, we all felt invulnerable in combat. If anyone was going to get hit, we all knew, *Doc's got me*. You proved that. Many times."

They might have felt invulnerable over there, but over here? Different story. Who was around to call on when the war was within themselves? When Doc wasn't around? "Maybe you're right."

"Fuck off with the maybe!" Porter exclaimed. "I've got five deployments under my belt to Iraq and Afghanistan. You think I don't know what I'm talking about?" Then calmly,

"Let's change the subject. How's California really treating you?"

"It's going alright, I guess."

"That's got to be a hell of a transition, going from what we went through and then going to school with a bunch of teenagers who don't know shit about fuck. All those years spent scraping your knuckles on the ground and actually doing something with your life. It's got to be hard to relate." Porter looked over at him, that tone back in his voice. "You know you can always call me if you need to. Just because we're no longer in theatre doesn't mean I'm going to stop looking out for ya."

Michael sighed. "Trust me, I know that." He took a deep inhale in, then slowly let it out. Paused. "I'm not used to asking for help."

"None of us are, Bubba. We are the help."

Michael thought about that for a minute, letting his gaze go back to the long line of trees along the highway. Thinking again how different things could have been for Porter if he'd gone through with it. Wondering how many phone calls he would have had to make to everyone he'd have left behind in the army. Angry with himself, he looked up to the sky and swore he'd do whatever he could to not go down that road again.

"Are you at least getting laid out there?"

"Yeah." Michael smiled. "But it's complicated."

"It always is until it isn't, Bub."

# CHAPTER 21

Michael slept at Porter's house that night. Woke to the smell of coffee brewing and bacon frying. Got cleaned up. In the kitchen, he gave Porter's young wife a hungover "Good morning" and a hug as a greeting, and she flashed a smile at him and returned the hug. He helped himself to some coffee and joined Porter at the dining room table, where he was already sipping on his. The men were served their breakfast in silence as they reflected and braced for the day to come.

After they finished eating Michael changed into the cheap suit that he'd bought for this occasion, applying a small silver pin to the suit jacket—an empty evac litter surrounded by a wreath and, in the middle, two snakes entwined around a staff that led to a winged cross above it. His combat medic badge. Porter changed into his dress uniform with all his awards and decorations displayed proudly across his chest, the blue infantry cord around his right shoulder. He balanced his beret on his head, said goodbye to his wife with a kiss, and the two climbed into his truck. It was a quiet drive to the funeral home.

The viewing was closed casket. The lights in the funeral parlor were low but plentiful, negating any shadows while giving the place a dusky feeling. Hushed voices filled the room as people exchanged idle conversation or filed by the coffin to pay their respects. An awkward, quiet laugh occasionally sounded from different corners as reunions occurred. Michael took note of who was there, who he recognized. Luke, Dusten, and Ned stood in a corner along with Pupalia. Hektar, now a captain, was closer to Michael, talking to a large, bearded man in a conspicuously expensive suit offset by Chuck Taylors. Tattoos flowed out of his shirt sleeves onto his hands and from his shirt collar onto his neck. When he made eye contact with Michael, he tilted his head up with a smile, opening up his suit jacket to reveal a bottle of Jameson.

"Thank God you're here, Ace," Michael said as he walked over and accepted the bottle. "Captain Hektar. On break from group?"

"I'm finishing up the language training in Monterrey, perfecting my Español. Figured I could take a weekend off from that," he responded, half frowning as Michael and Ace took turns drinking.

"No kidding? You've been in my neck of the woods and didn't think to call?"

Ace snorted. "Cap here is all business now, no time to waste with us peasants. Plus, he doesn't have time for fun while he's busy training to ship off to South America so he can interfere with my cocaine habit."

"Being a military contractor is obviously going well for you if you can afford a habit like that," Hektar said, sipping a glass of water.

"Four times the pay, a quarter of the bullshit. Gotta love it. Got my home in Tennessee, summer in Europe, and that aforementioned habit's only problem is that I either have too much of it or not enough. Then there is the benefit of not having to deal with the VA hospital system." He gestured at Conchord's coffin. "Obviously that alone is worth it."

Michael had heard the stories. Long wait times, exhausted doctors moving from complicated case to complicated case. Michael himself had applied for treatment and the first appointment he could get with his primary care provider was still months away. If they were doing the same things that they did for those on active duty, it would mean prescribing pills until the pain qualified for surgery. More like a slow death than treatment.

"You know." Ace perked back up with a swig from the bottle. "Screw Monterrey. Y'all should come with me. I'll show you a place like nothing you've ever experienced. Woman, wine, and an adrenal rush that'll give you a high like you're back in the bush taking pop shots from a Kalashnikov."

"I could be talked into it—I'll be on summer vacation for school—but sounds like Captain America here will be stacking bodies somewhere at that point. Where are you talking about?"

Michael was interrupted as the chaplain called the room to silence.

When the room calmed down, the priest went into a sermon. It was touching but felt tired as if he'd already given this speech a dozen times today. He then invited anyone up to share a few words on Conchord's behalf. A few family members came up. Shared stories about Conchord's courage, read Bible verses. Others talked about how much they had looked up to him. Ace was Conchord's best friend and had been at his side through several deployments, including the one where he had gotten wounded. He started talking about how good of a friend Conchord was, then trailed off, instead telling about the time the two of them were in a gunfight when a Kiowa gunship above them unloaded on the enemy and showered them with hot brass. A piece fell into Conchord's body armor at the neck, causing him to panic as though he'd been hit. Ace, staring at the casket, remarked that the way Conchord had just about danced in his frenzy was the funniest thing ever. A few laughed.

Michael chose not to say anything.

The chaplain then asked for the pallbearers to move the coffin. Michael, one of the six chosen, lifted the coffin in tandem with Ace, Porter, Dusten, Luke, and Ned. They carried it off to the waiting hearse outside, carefully loading the casket and shutting the doors. Each made their way to their vehicles and lined up behind the hearse to caravan to the grave site.

Michael rode with Porter, and Ace jumped into the truck along with them. They drove for a few minutes, following a winding route through the cemetery, until the hearse stopped by a freshly dug grave. They all parked in one big line, then Michael, Porter, and Ace got out to meet the other pallbearers behind the hearse. After opening its rear doors, Michael reached in on one side as Ace did the same on the other. Michael grabbed a handle and pulled. The pain in his neck flared, and it took everything he had not to cry out. Gritting his teeth, he held his end as they shuffled their way over to the grave as a group. Carefully they laid the coffin down. Michael noticed a few things missing.

"Is he not getting buried with full honors?" he whispered to Porter as they moved behind the rows of folding chairs and their scattering of occupants.

He shook his head. "They'll play taps, that's it. Command didn't want to glorify how he went out."

"I thought the investigation was still going on? So, what? They've already passed judgement and aren't giving him the burial he earned?"

Porter stared ahead at the casket. "Not going to lie to you, Bub, I'm on the fence about what he deserves. Those cops were just doing their job. Not like they get any training on how to deal with the crap he pulled. Now they have to live with his blood on their hands."

Michael nodded grimly, trying to ignore the searing electricity running through his neck and into his arms as the burial service went on. The chaplain said another prayer. Michael heard several people sobbing in front of him; more sobs joined in as they lowered Conchord down into the dirt. A soldier Michael didn't recognize started playing taps. Those in uniform who were still seated stood up and saluted. Michael felt awkward not being in uniform but joined them in the salute. The haunting notes of the bugle filled the air, causing his face to grimace, his eyes to water. The shooting pang in his neck peaked as he held his hand rigidly up to his right eyebrow. He held it in spite of the agony, focusing on his anger.

It could have been him in the dirt, doing this same thing to those he cared about.

# CHAPTER 22

The wake was at Conchord's old farmhouse, tucked away about twenty miles outside of Fort Campbell. It was an overgrown ten acres of planted ground and woods. Conchord's mother and father greeted everyone as they filed inside at the entrance to the house. Michael expressed his condolences; as he did, Conchord's father leaned in to let him know that he, along with anyone else who might need to, could stay the night. Michael thanked him for that, knowing full well that he and a bunch of the others would be tying one on tonight.

Food and drinks peppered the living room, and everyone mingled and chatted. People filtered in who weren't at the funeral as people who were at the funeral filtered out, a changing of the guard, while the core group kept their posts. Day turned to night as sharing memories turned into more airing of frustrations about the lack of care veterans got when coming home. At his limit, Michael wandered outside to the fire pit. Here, those who had had their hands on the coffin had started to congregate with a few others.

Ace passed beers around, demanding that everyone take one, practically forcing one into Captain Mallard's reluctant hand. "Alrighty, boys. One last toast to Conchord." Ace raised his beer, waiting for everyone to join him. "The fucking prick."

There was a muffled chorus of that last part as everyone took a drink. "What a fucked-up way to bring us all together," Michael said.

Porter nodded. "It's too bad we couldn't keep you here, but we all have to move on eventually. Not that it makes a difference. Always good to have my medic around." He slapped Michael on the back. "You too, Ace, but only in short intervals."

Ace quaffed. "You sound like all my ex's."

"Well, the truth is bound to be heard on repeat, Bubba." Porter grinned. "So what's good in your world? Where are you heading to next, ya merc?"

"I prefer the term soldier of fortune," Ace said, finishing his beer. "I'm on break for the next several months. Got that summer vacation planned that will blow your minds. Any of you ever been to Spain?"

"I have." Mallard said, and crossed his arms. "Let me guess, you're going to run with the bulls?"

"You know me well, sir."

"From what I remember, I had a good time. Did it before I started college after reading *The Sun Also Rises*. It was fun. Run was intense and over before I knew it."

"Kind of like Ace's first time?" Dusten chuckled, shaking Ace's shoulders.

"Kind of like your first gun fight," Ace shot back.

Mallard considered that. "You know, I'd say it actually was close to that as well."

"Just imagine eight days of waking up to that sensation, taking an afternoon nap, waking up to a nonstop party, chasing women all through the night, and starting it all over again the next morning. It's a paradise for functional alcoholic adrenaline junkies." Ace paused. "I had Conchord convinced to come with me this year. Then he decided to pull this shit instead."

Everyone got quiet. "He once told me that men like us are cursed," Michael said. "That we'd always be chasing that high we got in combat. Maybe if he would have gone, it would have prevented him from doing this crap. Hell, maybe something like that is what we all need in order to stay sane."

Mallard looked at him. "I think you should have more faith in yourself than that, Doc. You got a good life ahead of you. You've all got more good things ahead of you if you'll allow it. No need to go on a suicide run to get your rocks off."

Michael wondered if lectures like this were taught to officers as a standard response or if this was being regurgitated from some chaplain's speech.

Porter was next to him, nodding. "Faith and family. That's what really matters. Those right there get you through the dark times. Conchord? Cursed? Maybe with traumatic brain injury and PTSD."

He was backing up his commander, professional that he was, but Michael wondered if Porter fully agreed with him.

Mallard nodded. "I don't want to get preachy with you gentlemen, but faith in God has helped far more men like Conchord than chasing a high has. Might have been church and faith in God could have saved him from doing what he did"

"No offense, sir, but God is an absentee father in an empty house," Michael snapped. "I'm sorry, sir, but I've been to church, I've prayed, I've felt nothing there. After all we've seen and done, I'm not ready to believe it's all part of a master plan. Hell, I'd rather believe in curses and Taliban voodoo than God." He looked at Ace. "I'm in."

Ace raised his beer to him as Porter shook his head. "I disagree with you on that, but I don't think the bull run is a bad thing. I'm out though. I've got a baby on the way and I'm dropping retirement papers soon. You boys have fun with that white people shit."

Dusten, Luke, and Ned exchanged looks and nods. "Fuck it, we're in," Ned said for them. "If you grant us leave to do so, sir."

"I'll allow it. I don't agree with it, but you've all earned your right to do what you want with your free time," Mallard said reluctantly. "Just come back unharmed and without causing an international incident."

Hektar looked at Mallard. "Don't worry about it. I'll go and keep an eye on these heathens. I was already planning on going with Conchord when he told me about it."

"Then we've got six. Perfect," Ace said, grabbing a fresh beer. "Well, here's to Pamplona and fiesta, boys!"

The six formed a circle, crashing their cans together. Mallard and Porter stood in the back and raised their drinks to them.

"Cool," Luke said, and finished his beer. "So when is this thing?"

# CHAPTER 23

A little past midnight Michael took a walk away from the fire pit, shuffling toward the wooded area of the property. The trees opened up to a glade not too far from the house, and he stood there gazing up at the night sky, marveling at the brightness of the stars, the flickering specs of light all the more illuminated in the moonless night. He found Orion's belt and traced its lines toward Taurus. Michael lay down, ignoring the pain in his neck and propping himself on his elbows. He couldn't look away from the horns bearing down on Orion, a bullfight in the heavens.

He heard footsteps behind him, large ones that he recognized as Porter's. His gaze fell back down to look at Porter as he entered the glen, and he rubbed the back of his neck to help loosen the muscles.

"You okay, Bubba?" Porter asked, sidling up to Michael.

"Yeah. Got bulls on my mind."

"I think you and the boys are going to have an amazing experience." He got quiet for a bit. "I didn't want to tell you this, but I think one of the reasons Conchord went crazy is because he found out he was getting medically retired. The army was done with him, and he couldn't handle the idea of not being a soldier anymore. Was too much for him."

"Probably it isn't easy to let go when you dedicate your life to a thing and are told to move on from it. Maybe that's the real curse."

"Could be," Porter said, nodding along. "But what the captain said does have value. A little faith in a higher power can go a long way."

Michael gave a sideways glance. "I can't rationalize religion after being over there and seeing what it does to people. Seeing kids torn apart from blasts, ours and the enemy's. Where's God in all that? I'd rather put my faith in the sun and the moon. At least I can scientifically rationalize the effects those two have on the world." He pointed up at the night sky. "What we can actually see up there, that's what affects my reality." All the myths and fables the stars held... He wanted to believe that there might be some salvation in the mysticism that shone from their light.

"I'm not trying to convert you, Bubba. I've lived through a lot of crap, have seen all the same horrors you have and then some. I've had encounters that I know I shouldn't have lived through—hell, that I shouldn't have even walked away from. For whatever reason, I'm still here. I'm starting a family. Me? I'll count that a miracle any day of the week and feel blessed. I'm not saying you should go to church. Fuck, the only reason I go is because the baby momma drags me in. I've got my own relationship with God, the universe. Whatever you hippies out in California call it. But there is peace in saying fuck it and trusting in something greater than yourself."

"Thought we had alcohol for that."

Porter didn't laugh at that. "To tell you the truth I'm looking forward to putting the bottle down when we get out of here."

Michael studied his own empty beer.

Porter looked back up at the sky; Michael looked up at Porter, his large frame and dark skin an outline of a fatherly figure against the twinkling sky. Porter's eyes seemed to move to the same constellations. "It's not like this happened to me overnight. I've gone through the boozing and cursing God." He looked back down at Michael with eyes that shone through the darkness. "Maybe this trip to Spain will be good for you and the boys. A little adrenaline. A little life and love instead of death and destruction. Who knows? Maybe you'll find something out about yourself while you live it up."

"Or I'll get addicted to it like Ace."

"Maybe you'll find a little Spanish honey and bring her back."

"Maybe I'll find one and stay there." Michael watched the sky. "It's still got to be better than wishing I were back in Afghanistan."

Porter smiled weakly. "Just try and figure out what it is that you want. The rest will fall into place when you do." He leaned down and clapped Michael on his shoulder, then made his way back over to the others. Michael lay there for a few more moments, stealing glances at Taurus and Orion. After another ten minutes of contemplating the stars, he got up and joined the others in finding a place to lie down for the rest of the night.

# CHAPTER 24

Michael had been waiting at the diner for over thirty minutes. A week had gone by since Conchord's funeral and he had been thinking about what Porter had told him. He'd been sober since that night and was now fulfilling his monthly meet-up obligation with his father, per his request. Every time they met, he struggled more and more to keep their relationship on neutral ground. He was sitting in a back corner booth, alternating between looking at his quarter-empty coffee mug and out the big windows overlooking the parking lot. The diner had that cozy feeling, the kind that you can find in any small town. Family owned and operated, staff who treated everyone with friendly recognition, even Michael. He'd grown up coming to this place, and while he didn't remember the names and they didn't remember his, he was welcomed as a local.

His father, frequently late for these meals, seemed to take more time to arrive the more time that passed since his leaving the army. He was getting ready to ask for the bill and pay for his coffee when he finally saw his father's decade-old used corvette swing into the parking lot. Michael looked at his watch to confirm how long he had been waiting, politely declining the refill the waitress offered. Instead, he asked her for a cup of water.

He watched as his father approached the diner entrance, dressed in a golf polo tucked into slacks that did nothing but enhance his potbelly. The wear of the outfit looked like he might have slept in them or worn them already yesterday; his hair and beard looked unkempt as well. The way he walked, Michael suspected he'd probably already had an early cocktail or two.

Michael wore his irritation on his face; his father ignored it and sat down.

"How was Tennessee?" His breath confirmed Michael's suspicions.

"It was a funeral, so not that great."

His father shifted his weight to be more midline in the booth, raising a hand as he did to get the waitress's attention. "Can I get a chardonnay?" he asked as she arrived with Michael's water. When he lowered his hand, Michael saw the tan line on the ring finger.

His father sighed. "I told you for years you should get out. But you had to be like your uncles. Had to be like your grandfather, trying to make a career out of it."

"I remember you trying to make a career out of it."

"Never. I went in because it was expected of me." He sank back in the booth. "Now I've earned more money than both your uncles combined. Which is why I don't understand why you chose to be like them."

Michael appraised his father. When he was young, he wore cowboy boots—would hunt, fish, work with his hands. Everyone had regarded him as a man's man. When Michael grew to become a teenager, his father sold off his construction company, putting away a quick million, then divorced his mother, who in turn took her profits from the divorce and now traveled full time. These days, his father seemed to have morphed into a lazy middle-class pseudo-intellectual who sustained himself by marrying and divorcing wealthy divorcees, each new wife richer than the last.

The chardonnay finally arrived and his father hastily took a swallow. "Look, son, nobody on this planet loves you more than I do. And I think maybe it's time you listen to me, quit messing around, and get a job."

"I do have a job. Going to school and working toward a career is my job." Michael stared at his father's empty ring finger.

His father pulled his left hand under the table. "That's not a job. That's exactly your problem. You haven't the faintest how to work for a living."

"I guess all those years in the army don't qualify as working for a living."

"You know what I mean."

"No, I really don't."

Why did he bother meeting him? The conversation was always the same. They would sit here, his father passing judgement until he'd had enough to drink to be put in a good mood. Then he would talk about them doing something fun together. Golfing or fishing. Plans that never came to fruition. His father would golf and fish, of course; he just never extended Michael an invite. The rare times he did, Michael showed, only to discover his father absent, to call him to find out he'd gone on some lavish vacation and forgotten their plans. Michael was rolling back over the line *Nobody on this planet loves you more than I do* when the waitress came by and refilled Michael's coffee.

"What are your plans for summer, then? Since you won't be working."

Michael came back from his apathy. "The guys and I are going to Spain to do the Running of the Bulls."

"What?!"

Michael stiffened. "Me and a bunch of the guys who were at Conchord's funeral are going to fly to Spain to see the bull run."

His father squinted his eyes at him. "What the fuck is wrong with you?" He leaned forward as if he might find his answer in Michael's eyes, hands guarding the wine glass in front of him.

Michael noticed that his gold wedding ring had returned to his finger. "What do you mean?"

"You just came back from your soldier buddy's funeral, a boy who killed himself, and now—what? To honor him, you and a couple of other guys are going to try and do the same?"

"It's not like that. Why the fuck would you say it like that?"

"Then what's it like? I thought you were going to come back here and chill out. Be normal. Instead, you're going to fly off again and get yourself killed doing some more dumb shit."

Normal. Michael saw red. Hadn't he been trying to live a normal life?

His father sat back again. "Honestly, I don't know why you even bothered to get out if this is how you're going to act."

"You begged me to get out!" Michael practically yelled at him.

The diner got quiet. Patrons and staff looked over at them. Voice lowered, Michael went on "You've been begging me to get out ever since my first tour, telling me all about the stress I've caused you by being over there, and now that you finally have what you wanted, this is how you treat me?"

"I'm treating you like a man, if only you'd grow up, little boy."

Michael gripped the coffee mug and debated its use as a projectile. The seconds ticked by as they sat and glared at each other, neither wanting to give in. Michael, hyperaware of the stares and whispers around them, eased his grip on the mug. "You know what? I'm just going to go." He stood up, pulled out his wallet, and dropped a twenty-dollar bill on the table.

"Yeah, just go." Then quietly, "Go get yourself checked out, son, because you're not right."

Michael kept his composure as he left the diner and got into his truck. Drove a few blocks away, then pulled into an empty parking lot. Then he broke, punching his fist into the dash and center console, screaming as he did so. Letting the anger and rage take him over. Hyperventilating. Slowly, he did his best to regain control, calming his breathing down and letting his heart rate settle, but when that familiar grip in his chest, frigid and unyielding, seized him, he ripped open the center console, yanking the bottle from its spot in a flurry and splashing the liquid down his throat. He waited while the whiskey worked its way through his nervous system, taking in several deep breaths. Another deep inhale and exhale. The grip released, gradually, like fingers being plucked from a forbidden treasure. Soon, he was in control enough of his faculties to put the bottle back.

He took out a stick of gum. Chewed it to get the alcohol off his breath. Thought to check his surroundings. His tantrum, it seemed, hadn't alerted anyone around him.

He looked over at the glovebox for a long moment. "No. Fuck that, and fuck him." He put the truck into drive and pulled out of the parking lot.

Not ready to go home, he drove randomly, avoiding stopping at any point, turning here and there to avoid losing momentum. He pumped his fist to loosen it up from pounding it into the center console, letting the blood flow in and out. The fury simmered there still. He had let his father get to him, something he'd been allowing him to do for years. He had let his father push him so hard he'd broken his sober streak. His father, who was likely headed back to his cozy home with wife number three, or maybe back to his mistress's house. Judging him from a throne built of lies and immorality.

Michael sat back farther into the driver's seat. That PTSD label his father had plastered on him when he got back? It was just his way of controlling him.

He turned on his radio to focus on something else. He found a classic rock station, the only station number that he remembered and that hadn't changed from his years abroad. The noise came through his truck's speakers right in the middle of a song. Michael recognized it immediately, the samba beat and lyrics.

*'Cause I'm in need of some restraint.*

The upbeat, fun, and happy melody contradicting the song's dark and morbid words was a strange comfort. He wished he could start the song over and listen from the beginning. As "Sympathy for the Devil" finished, he turned down a street from his childhood; ahead of him he could see his old elementary school and the church steeple next to it. It was a private Catholic school that he had attended for several years, and he felt compelled to pull into the parking lot. Nostalgia took him as he parked. He was baptized at this church, went through First Penance and Confirmation here. He couldn't remember the last time he had gone to confession—likely for some special occasion under force from his parents. That all stopped when they got divorced and sent him to public school. "Guess divorces are too expensive to maintain stability for your child," he said to himself, and got out of his truck.

In front of him was the church; to his left the school. On his right was the apple orchard he'd always remembered being here. Small orderly gardens and religious figurines guarded the church on both sides. He reached a hand to open one of the large double-doors to let himself in and found that it was locked. He tried the other side. Locked as well. Michael sighed and shook his head, thinking about what Captain Mallard had talked about, then dismissing entirely the idea of going into the church.

His gaze drifted to the apple orchard. The fruit was in full bloom, ready to be plucked. He stopped in front of the first tree and admired the bright red fruit against the dull brown and green of the tree, all set against the light blue sky. The sun was out, a beautiful day despite the earlier meeting with his father. He thought about those song lyrics, this place seeming appropriate to reflect on them. He wondered if Lucifer had a similar problem with his father. Was that why he was cast out? He certainly felt that. A forgotten son passed aside for the next interest, used as a scapegoat for all the problems in this world, then sent to hell. He wondered if the devil had created his own paradise. What was that saying? One man's hell is another's heaven? Looking at the apple tree backdropped by the California mountains reminded him bleakly of Afghanistan, of the better life he'd left there.

"It's okay, feel free to take an apple."

Michael whipped his head around, a twang of pain rising; he'd been lost in the trees and hadn't heard the man approach. "I'm sorry. I was just looking."

The man was wearing blue jeans and a dark green button-down shirt with all the stains befitting the ensemble of a gardener. He was shorter than him, stocky and well-tanned, with high cheek bones and brown eyes that glinted in the sunlight. Vietnamese, likely.

"No need to apologize. This is my family's orchard." His voice had a song-like quality pleasant to the ears. "We're getting ready to harvest soon."

Michael stood there for a moment, then nodded to the gardener. He reached out his left hand to grab a ripe red apple that looked almost ready to drop on its own. One twist, and it came away easy in his hand. He pulled it toward him and wiped it off on his shirt, looking at the gardener. "Thanks. I was just taking a walk and thinking to myself"

The man chuckled. "It's a good place for it. I saw you standing here and thought you could use an apple. My name is Ra." He held out a hand and Michael gripped it, the hand-shake firm. His silver watch glinted, its Rolex emblem apparent.

"Great to meet you, Ra. I'm Michael," he said, and pointed to his wrist. "Nice watch."

"Thanks." Ra tilted it in the sunlight. "It was a gift from a friend of mine."

"That's an expensive gift."

He laughed. "I know. He was a good man. He helped bring my family over from Vietnam." He smiled and looked out over the trees. "He was a soldier. I served with him when I was a little boy."

"A little boy?"

"Yes, in my culture, you're a man much earlier than here. Something I've had to adapt to as my family and I have become American." He recognized Michael's interest. "My friend was in your Special Forces. Him and his own trained my people to fight the Vietcong. When the war ended, he helped bring my family over. Then he gave me this watch as a present." He chuckled to himself. "He was a good man, but he ended up going back to Vietnam. I haven't heard from him in a long time, but I hope he is still alive and that he found happiness." Ra looked at Michael and gestured to the band on his wrist. "Seems you might have an idea of what I'm talking about."

Michael rubbed the band and thought about the interpreters and Afghans he fought alongside, still in their own country. He wondered if he could go back.

"Is that what you were thinking about out here?"

"Something like that." Michael thought for a moment. "Do you miss Vietnam?"

"Sometimes, but my life here is great. I have a good family. Those were..." He looked off into the distance. "Hard times. Hard times that my children won't ever have to deal with because I've come here and stayed here."

Michael thought about this, too, mind still on Afghanistan. "So I guess you found paradise here. Your friend, he found paradise in Vietnam?"

He shrugged. "Hard to say. He traveled a lot after he brought us over here. The last thing he said was that he wanted to go back to Vietnam. He said life made more sense to him over there."

Michael looked at him. "I think I can relate. Do you think the travel helped him?"

Ra looked contemplative. "He always had exciting stories about all the places he went to. I think that helped him feel good."

Michael perked up with that news. "I've got travel plans of my own coming up."

Ra grinned kindly. "Oh? To where?"

"My friends from the army and I are going to Spain to go running with the bulls."

Ra shook his head with a smile. "I have heard of this and I don't understand. In my country we have water buffalo. Docile creatures. I used to lead them as a small boy." He looked up at the apple tree. "We had ceremonies to honor them. We had a..." He paused, seemingly searching for a word. "A medicine man, and we'd sacrifice a bull to the gods to help us with battle."

Michael hadn't known this. "I guess bulls are important all over the world."

Ra nodded. "Very important. Just look in the sky at night."

Michael chuckled to himself, thinking about his experience at

Conchord's a few weeks ago and looking up, letting the sun hit his face. "I agree. Very important."

Ra looked at his watch, then back to Michael. "You'll have to come back and tell me about the bull run. My house is there." He pointed to the far side of the orchard. "You are welcome anytime, Michael."

"I'll take you up on that offer, Ra, and you can tell me more stories about your friend."

"I would enjoy that very much. You enjoy the apple; they are very good."

Michael stood admiring the trees after Ra left him, twirling the apple in his hand under the shining sun. He was still angry about his encounter with his father but now held what felt a healthy strength and optimistic defiance. His encounter with Ra had him looking forward to the future, giving him more things to contemplate prior to leaving for Spain.

He took a bite out of the apple. Ra was right; the apple was good.

## Chapter Twenty-Six

With the festivities in Pamplona starting on the sixth, it gave him the chance to spend the Fourth of July in his hometown before flying out that night. American flags had spontaneously sprouted all over every window shop and lamppost. Adults dressed themselves and their kids in patriotic apparel. Children waved their miniature flags excitedly only to discard them along the sidewalks as soon as they no longer held their attention. All of it for one day.

Nostalgia couldn't help but hit him as he moved along the streets following the parade to meet Kent and his girlfriend. Memories hit of him with his mother, trailing after the horses from her equestrian club, both dressed as clowns cleaning up the mess as they cantered through the streets. Looking around at the line of floats and cars, he didn't see any animals or any of the old country comforts once a staple of the parade. The rural country vibe previously prevalent here had been absorbed by the influence of the technocrats from the Bay Area, his home a conquered version of what he remembered. Feeling out of place, he moved along quickly.

A few blocks down he found Kent standing next to a cooler on wheels on which a pretty, petite blonde with light blue eyes sat.

"Michael, you old war hero! Happy Fourth of July!" He greeted Michael with a hug. "Meet my girlfriend, Heide. I've told her all about you."

Shrugging off the hero comment, Michael accepted the hug and turned to accept Heide's extended hand as she turned in her seat. "Nice to meet you. Hopefully he didn't tell you everything."

She smiled, but there was something else behind her eyes that Michael couldn't quite read. "I already knew enough, I think."

"Okay." He chuckled awkwardly. "What's that supposed to mean?"

Heide shrugged her shoulders. "I'm friends with Evelyn. I heard more about you from her."

Michael looked at Kent, who was busy looking at the parade. "I'm not sure what you're getting at here."

His tone and the look on his face caused her to backpedal a bit. "I'm sorry, I just meant that you should leave her alone."

"I haven't seen her or spoken to her in months. What does she want me to do? Move to a new town?"

"Well, if you're going to act like a stalker, then maybe."

"I just said I haven't seen or spoken to her, so what are you accusing me of?"

"Nothing, I'm only going off of what I've heard about you."

"Babe!" Kent finally jumped in. "It's the Fourth of July, this guy spent a decade in service to our country, cut him some slack. Besides, you know how Evelyn is. Now scoot your butt; I'm getting Michael a drink."

"How she is?" She got up and Kent rummaged through the cooler. "She's single and enjoying her life. After the bullshit she's gone through, she has that right. Don't be an asshole."

It seemed there might have been some truth to what Evelyn had told him. "Look, she and I both wanted different things, that's all. And I get it. We live in a small town. Things get shared. But the stalker thing is bullshit."

"That's not how she told it." She looked away from him toward the parade.

"I'm not playing this game," Michael said as he accepted a beer concealed in a koozie from Kent. "It's been too long since I've seen her to have to listen to this crap. You can tell her that I haven't said anything about her and I'm not looking to start anything, so let's stop with the he said, she said bullshit and move along with our lives, yeah?"

"Amen to that," Kent said, toasting Michael.

They went quiet and turned to the parade. Eventually, more polite small talk started between the three as the flotillas and town officials went by on classic cars. Michael calmed down as he emptied his beer and had it replaced as soon as it ran dry. Kent caught up on the latest from Michael, and the conversation turned to his plans for the rest of the week.

"Actually, I'm flying out tonight to go to Spain."

Heide perked up at that comment. "Oh! I love Spain; where are you going?"

"Pamplona. I'm meeting some of my army buddies to go do the Running of the Bulls."

"I've always wanted to do that!" Kent exclaimed. "You should have told me, I would have gone."

"Like hell you would have gone," Heide said with a frown

"It was a last-minute thing that we put together," Michael offered as an apology to Kent.

Heide was still frowning. "I know you guys hunt, but doesn't that whole bull running, bullfighting thing fall under animal cruelty?"

Michael shrugged. "Honestly, I haven't even thought about it. It just looks fun and dumb to me."

"I know they do have the bullfights afterwards," Kent said, sipping his beer. "I've always been curious about that. They used to have them in the old rodeo arena in town, something like thirty, forty—hell, maybe fifty years ago. My old man used to talk about it."

Heide threw her arms out wide. "Now that is nothing but animal cruelty. What purpose could that have other than sick entertainment value?" She regarded both of them brashly.

"I'm pretty sure none of the meat gets wasted," Kent said as an explanation. "But I don't know."

Michael shrugged. "I've been to enough countries with weird shit going on that I don't agree with. I'm not going over there to change anything; I think I've already tried that. If you only knew some of the cultural practices in Afghanistan, a bullfight wouldn't sound harmful at all. I'm going to have a good time and to see what the fuss is about."

"So because it's not the most horrific thing you'll see in your life, it's okay?" Heide asked, folding her arms.

"What I'm getting at is I don't know enough about it to pass judgement. I'm not the kind of person to simply take it on what someone else says to form an opinion on a thing." Michael looked at Heide. "Or on a person."

"That seems like an excuse to not have any morals."

"How about we enjoy the parade?" Kent desperately wanted to keep the peace. "It is the Fourth of July. Let's drink some beers and try to come together as Americans."

Michael sighed and they got quiet again as the town's mayor road past them on an older model Cadillac. A plastic-looking man with a practiced plastic smile. Independence Day in his hometown had lost the excitement he remembered of it from his childhood. Everyone would celebrate their country for just one day, then go back to normal. Meanwhile he was about to go to a town in Spain that would celebrate for over a week.

"I still think it should be banned," Heide said, shattering the silence.

"Guess I should get there before you get your way," Michael growled. He turned his head back to the parade, neck hurting from craning it to watch. Every action he'd taken since he moved back here seemed to be contrary to someone else's point of view. Michael wondered if this *normalcy* that everyone wanted him to conform to was beyond his scope of thinking now. Looking forward, he thought about Pamplona and the life and death spectacle that he was bound to see.

Maybe it was the type of place where he belonged.

# CHAPTER 25

The next day, Michael looked out at Manhattan Island through an airport window tucked away in the expansive international terminal. He was killing time until the rest of the group flew in from their respective parts of the country. Everyone except Ace and Hektar had scheduled flights that converged in New York to connect to Spain.

This was his first time here. Seeing the skyline stirred up a curious mix of emotions. Michael picked out One World Tower. He imagined how different the scene would look if the Twin Towers still stood. He remembered his father shaking him awake, telling him he needed to see something. It was his tone that got him out of bed so early that Tuesday morning with no complaint, and he sat and watched the events of September 11, 2001, unfold from the other side of the country. Though barely in high school, he knew somehow, at that moment, that his life would be forever changed. His life and so many others, sent off to protect freedom or enact revenge?

Looking at the skyline he tried to think if he had known of anyone who had been there during the attacks. The whole world shook that day, a few extremists causing repercussions across the globe.

Shaken, that icy grip sneaking up around his heart, he hurried off to find a bar somewhere in the terminal. He finally found one, the view of the New York skyline visible out a nearby window, and impatiently raised a hand to the bartender to get his attention. He ordered a shot of whiskey and a beer. The bartender took his time as he poured him the beer. Michael watched critically as the bartender then put a glass in front of him and poured a small splash of whiskey.

Holding up the poor excuse of a shot in disbelief, Michael scoffed. "My man! How about you poor me a real shot?"

"That'll be double."

"Whatever, just pour it," he said, staring angrily as the bartender poured something more suitable to Michael's needs. "Thank you." His eyes followed the bartender as he walked away without any acknowledgment.

Draining the shot, he couldn't help thinking, *Is this the type of asshole my friends and I sacrificed so much for?* Had he gone to the other side of the world to fight and die for people like this? Maybe it really should have been a mission of revenge rather than the pseudo-training arena it became like Conchord and Porter said. Just gone in, fucked things up, and gotten out of there.

He remembered September 12 and the weeks and months that followed, how the patriotic fervor gripped everyone in the country. How many of those *Never Forget* murals were now fading or painted over? Was fervor all it was? Was that the reason he took off at eighteen to go to the other side of the globe? He wondered what would happen if he told the bartender he was a veteran. Would his attitude change? Would he hear a "Thank you for your service" and get a change in attitude? Maybe a free drink? Or would the thank you have the emotional backing of a "Bless you" after someone sneezed?

Michael thought about his uncles, about what they would they say. They were both of the Vietnam-era generation. Hadn't that conflict demonstrated the failures of nation-building? What about those Veterans who came home? The ones who were spit on, called baby killer after being drafted with their choice being go to war or go to jail. Those guys never got a thank you when they got home; it wasn't until recently that they could go out in public with their Vietnam Veteran hats on. He knew one veteran who didn't tell his wife he had been in Vietnam until fifteen years into their marriage.

He looked back at the bartender, ordered another beer, and calmed himself down. His back to the skyline, he looked at the people coming and going. Moving on with their lives oblivious to the debate in his mind, oblivious to what he had done, what he had gone through, what his whole generation had sacrificed. Oblivious to the fact that a war still raged, in his head and across the globe, as they scurried around. Paddocked cattle, concerned only with what was in front of them.

Jealous, Michael imagined himself back in Afghanistan, living on a binary scale, worrying only about life and death. It had been so simple, so freeing. Now, more than ever, he missed it. Sure, he'd had restrictions. Had in a way been fenced. But Conchord understood the freedom in it, and now Michael thought he did too.

He thought he had accepted death, that he no longer feared it, but looking at all these people, he wondered if he feared something else. Something worse. A few cautious glances slipped his way as he watched the crowd. Eyes scanned him as though he was a predator that had crept into their pen. His mere presence unsettled them. Maybe that was why the bartender snubbed him on the drink. Maybe it was now a permanent feature, a look or a brand the domesticated types subconsciously knew to give a wide berth. He smiled and shook his head, thinking about his time with Lilith, her suggestion to get help.

He turned back to face the bar and the city. Now he wished that he could go out into the streets and see Ground Zero. He waved the bartender over, asking for another shot and his tab. The drink still didn't meet his standard, but he accepted it without complaint. After paying his tab and snubbing the bartender on his tip, he turned and started walking toward his connecting flight and his brothers-in-arms, stealing one last glance over his shoulder at the tower and the entire New York skyline.

# PART FIVE
# TERCIO DE MUERTE

*"The mark of the immature man is that he wants to die nobly for a cause, while the mark of the mature man is that he wants to live humbly for one."*
—J.D. Salinger

# CHAPTER 26

Hektar and Ace were already in Pamplona; Michael and the other three landed in Madrid early on the sixth of July. Grabbing their luggage full of white shirts, pants, and throwaway shoes, they navigated to the bus station. Miraculously, they managed to get on the first bus to Pamplona. They were warned that they needed to get there well before noon, as the city would turn into a madhouse. Jet-lagged, hungover, and sleep deprived, the four boarded the bus, soon fully packed. Michael and Ned grabbed seats toward the back, and Dusten and Luke took seats in the aisle across from them. Michael got comfortable, letting his head slink into the window with a shoulder pressed against the latch, settling down for a nap despite the discomfort and the excited voices from all over the world that filled the bus.

He woke about several hours later as their bus pulled into the station, going underground into a modern parking structure that felt like a grave. The four unloaded in the dim light, trying to get their bearings. It was only a couple of hours before noon; they needed to get a move on. They followed the instructions Ace had sent, following signs to Plaza del Castillo into the older part of town. Modern buildings turned more ancient as the roads went from broad to narrow, like they were exiting the modern world and moving to something more artistic, more archaic. They found the plaza, already crowded with people wearing white. Using landmarks such as Hotel La Perla, they wove through the streets to an apartment on Aldapa where Ace and Hektar were waiting for them, and buzzed the apartment. They were let in with a warm greeting from a rosy-faced Ace holding a bright red bottle marked Pacharán.

"Bienvenidos to fiesta, fuckers! Time to get out of those American clothes and into some Sanfermines shit!" he announced, dropping the bottle into Michael's hand. Both he and Hektar were already dressed in all white and donning red sashes on their wrists.

"We've got rooms where you can change," Hektar explained as Michael took a sip of the intense yet sweet liquor. It sat in his stomach atop the sangria from the plastic magnum he had been working on. "We're here for the duration so don't be in a rush to black out on the first night like this guy," he added with a gesture toward Ace.

"Fuck you, this ain't my first rodeo. You guys do need to hurry up and change; Chupinazo starts soon. Shit's about to get wild." Ace took the bottle back from the new arrivals as they went to change.

Fifteen minutes later all of them were in uniform. They had their neckerchiefs that Ace encouraged them to call their pañuelos tied around their wrists. "You got to wait for Chupinazo, the start of fiesta," he gave as an explanation.

A horde of people had formed in the streets outside their door. Ace dove in, working to lead them all to the town square. They followed, armed with plastic bottles of Sangria in both hands, and fought through the crowd to get directly in front of the Ayuntamiento, a very regal-looking building with flags jutting out from its center. Sangria splashing and sprayed all around them. Giant beach balls bounced around, amusing everyone who came into contact with one. Women sat on boyfriends' shoulders, flashing the crowd only to be hosed down with more sangria and groped by those in reach. The combination of heat and sticky sweet alcohol soon had the crowd soaked, staining everyone in the area purple as they waited, surging back and forth as those in the crowd pushed and pulled to fill every possible cranny of the open square with more bodies.

Drunk off anticipation and the emotions of those around him, Michael tensed up, at first constricted by all the bodies and the overwhelming sights around him. Soon though, with the help of the alcohol, a comfort settled upon him. Something about being surrounded by everyone celebrating in the same uniform, like he was on the winning side of a sports team, had him lost in the moment and revelry.

His eyes rose up to the balcony of the old-world building. Cheers went up in the crowd as people appeared there. A chant began—*"San Fermin, San Fermin, San Fermin!"*—as everyone pulled their pañuelos out of their pockets, folded in half to form a triangle. They held their neckerchiefs aloft, stretched out between two hands. Someone important stepped up to a microphone on the balcony as everyone fought to remain on their feet while holding their pañuelos in the air like offerings.

"Pamploneses, pamplonesas, ¡Viva san Fermín! Gora San Fermín!" With that announcement, rockets fired into the air to the jubilation of the people around him. Copying the crowd, Michael tied his pañuelo around his neck as a brass band started up from inside the building. The crowd kept chanting, undulating, as the band moved into them, guided by police officers who inched everyone back, parting the throngs of people to make way for the musicians and their heavy brass instruments.

It took a long time for the band to clear the square and move down the street. People followed them as they marched on, while Michael and the rest of his posse stayed behind and moved to a less congested area where they could catch their breath. He looked toward the street where the band had gone with the people dancing behind it. "Well, that's one hell of a way to get a party started."

The following hours were a blur of drinking, dancing, laughing, flirting, and hopping from bar to bar sampling tapas and beverages. At one point, they found themselves in front of a fifteen-foot-tall fountain. Michael watched as a young man climbed it. Below him his friends cheered him on in Australian accents. As the twenty-something-year-old crested the top, his friends linked arms below, taunting him to dive down to them. Beer cans and plastic cups flew at the man as he hesitated at the top. Then he jumped, swan diving into his friends below, who somehow caught him.

Michael shook his head, hoping a medical team was close by in case someone else tried it and didn't get so lucky. He urged his group to move on; he didn't want old instincts to kick in if someone didn't make the jump.

As the crowds surged to different areas of the town or others settled down for an afternoon nap, Ace gathered them together, herding the belligerents like cats. "Time to show you the ropes, gentlemen." He moved them downhill on a one-lane road, then took them up some stone stairs to a small overlook surrounding a museum. They moved forward to a wall overlooking the street, a river and mountains off in the distance. An ancient walled city in the north of Spain. Below them across the street, in a wooden coral, they saw the bulls.

"Okay, boys, listen up," Ace started lecturing once he had everyone gathered in close enough to take in the scenery amid the crowd. "Down there are the bulls. I know some of you city boys have probably never seen anything other than a dairy cow on television, so take a good look. You see the bigger ones? Those are steers. They'll have them running with the wild bulls every day, keeping them on course. They wear bells around their necks so you'll hear them coming and be able to tell them apart from the fighting bulls, the Toros Bravos. You shouldn't have to worry about the steers; they run the route every day and are domesticated. That being said, don't do anything stupid that'll piss them off. That's still a big animal that can do a lot of hurt if you don't respect it. Now you see the smaller ones? Those are the real killers."

Michael nudged Ned at that comment.

"Six steers and six fighting bulls run every morning."

Luke burped. "One for each of us."

"Sure, if we do math your way." Ace gave an exaggerated inhale. "But let's remember that they aren't to be messed with. Also, don't try to touch them. You could be fined. It's pretty hard for them to enforce that when everyone is practically trying to do it, but try to avoid it. Now your first time is going to be—"

"—a lot like losing your virginity," Dusten jumped in. "And probably smells just like Ace's first time."

Ned and Luke snickered as Ace continued.

"Your first time, you're just happy to be there. Point is, don't try anything fancy. Get in and get it done. You boys aren't wearing body armor and those killers aren't slinging lead. The best way to stay alive and avoid injury is to stay on your feet. Chances are, though, you're going to get knocked on your asses by everyone else who saunters out there with no clue what they're doing. On that note, *ASSHOLES*, if you fall down, stay down. Don't try to get up. Wait for someone to pull you up or until you're absolutely sure there're no more bulls coming. The bulls' horns sit at the perfect height to gore you right in the vitals if you're on your knees."

Hektar, leaning over the wall to study the bulls, said, "The best way to stay alive is to sleep in."

"Pfft, that's nonsense coming from a warfighter," Ace spat. "Keep on your feet and keep moving. You want to *run* with the bulls! Become part of the herd. You don't want to become a highlight by dying from the bulls or falling in front of the bulls. The goal is to run with them. Then, when you grow up big and strong and have an idea about what you're doing out there, you might find yourself leading the herd through a section. That's the ultimate goal of this thing."

Michael cocked an eyebrow. "So tomorrow a bunch of drunks are going to try to lead these things up the streets?"

Ace looked at him. "You'll be sober, trust me. Adrenaline is a major hangover cure and the true runners, the Basque people, treat this like a religious experience. Plus, if you're too drunk the police will kick you out, and trust me, they have no problem going full Rodney King if you want to argue."

Luke looked at Ace. "Do we have to sign a waiver for this thing or how does it work?"

"Waivers? This is Spain. They don't create laws based on you willing to do something stupid. All you have to do is show up."

Dusten squinted. "There's more paperwork to go to war than to run with wild bulls."

Ace took a drink. "We've got eight chances, eight days of eight runs, to do this, so let's go over the route."

He led them down a narrow staircase to the street below them, taking them downhill toward where they'd seen the bulls. "The bulls will be released from the paddock there and led uphill back toward the town square. When the bulls are released, you'll hear a rocket. That goes off at 8 am. They shoot off a second rocket when all of the bulls have crossed that line." He pointed down to a mark on the street. "They'll shoot off a third rocket when they release a couple of clean-up steers to herd any sueltos. Things get really dangerous when a lone bull gets separated from the herd. The fourth rocket means that the bulls have all entered the arena. Count the rockets if you can." Ace paused. "You want to pay attention for them to go off so you can do what you need to do. Things are going to be pretty chaotic, so use whatever analogy works for your brains to remember them."

"What if we decide to bail and jump the fence?" Dusten asked.

"I'll make fun of you for the rest of your life," Ace responded. "That, and depending on where you try to bail, you might get tossed back over the fence. They have medics on standby at certain points, and they like to keep those areas clear for anyone who gets fucked up, so don't be a coward."

"I'm not worried. We've got our own trusty medic. I'm ready to push him in front of me if things get sketchy." Dusten splashed some Sangria on Michael. "Some of us have real jobs and have to get back in one piece. Plus, that always was your responsibility."

"I quit that job, remember?" Michael returned the splash. "My days of saving your sorry asses are over. No, I'm happy to sit on the fence and watch somebody else plug up any new holes you might get."

"Now we know how you really feel, Doc. Good thing we won't need you." Ace splashed some of his sangria on him as though feeling left out. "Gist is, stay on your feet and keep moving. Alright. Now I'ma show ya'll the rest of the route."

With that, they left the start of the route and moved up Santo Domingo, stopping again near Plaza del Ayuntamiento. "Tomorrow morning there will be barricades set up that'll funnel the herd from this street and turn them here, in front of the Ayuntamiento." Ace pointed to his right. "Wooden barricades will help lead them down the street at the turn down there, but closer to us in the square, the route opens up. This right here is a good spot to start, almost to the top of this hill, then run as the herd turns, leading the bulls through the square. Since it's open and barricaded there's great spots to get out of the way if you stay on either side of the route. Plus, by starting on the hill, with a view of the bottom, you can keep an eye out for the herd as it approaches so you'll know when it's time to move." Ace then led the group down the street past the Ayuntamiento. On their left, Michael saw a Burger King packed with revelers.

"That's a solid marketing choice for Burger King don't you think?" he said to the group as they passed it.

"Got to love capitalism, they knew what they were doing by opening a location on the run route," Ace said as he led them about fifty feet past the restaurant. "Now *this*—this is La Curva. Some call it the Curve of Death, although I don't think anyone's died here. Still, this is where you don't want to be. There will be a barrier here blocking the rest of the street in order to funnel the bulls up toward the arena. It's the sharpest turn on the route, and the bulls sometimes don't factor it right and slam against the wall at full speed. A great place to get your nuts caught up between a bull and a wall. People also like to pile up on the inside of the turn." Ace stopped and put a hand on the corner of the building where the streets crossed. "They like to stand here as the bulls pass by, and they tend to get pushy, so it's best to avoid this area."

"Those people who stand here, then—they're amateurs?" Michael asked.

"They're those with a death wish or who don't know what they're doing." Ace responded. "It can be done, but you need to really understand what's going on to master this section." Ace pointed behind him, at a painting of Saint Fermin on the wall of the building behind him. "There's a reason San Fermin watches over this area. Best not to leave things to divine intervention. I should also mention the pastores; they'll be in green and holding long poles to keep the bulls moving along the route." He flicked Michael's ear. "And to save your ass if you get into trouble."

Michael looked at the painting. "Sounds fun."

"Chill, Doc. Get your feet wet before taking on more than you can handle." Ace led them past La Curva. "Up here we got the long stretch." A narrow street, crowded with people. They struggled through it. They did their best to not step on crushed plastic cups, bump into people, or track through piles of vomit. Ace yelled to be heard as they waded through the crowd. "This is the longest stretch, so if you've got the legs for it, this can be a lot of fun." Ace continued on up the street until it opened into a clearing; ahead of them was the bullring. "It widens a bit again here so you have room to maneuver. The cool thing about starting up here is that you can lead the bulls into the arena or follow them in. This spot has a tendency to get packed, and usually some or a bunch of assholes fall down." He considered what he'd said. "Actually, that's true of the whole thing, which complicates things."

"This isn't that long of a route. Why not start at the beginning?" Dusten asked.

"These animals will be at a dead sprint and you'll get gassed quick, so it's better to pick a section, have your fun, then get out of the way. If the bulls don't get messed with, they'll do this whole thing in about two minutes. If you can hold a dead sprint for that long with a bunch of idiots falling down in front of you, then you should be hurdling in the Olympics, not doing dumb shit for the U.S. government."

"That's definitely not you," Dusten said, nudging Luke.

"What's not me?"

Ace narrowed his eyes at Luke. "Have you been paying attention to anything we've been talking about?"

"Yeah. Bulls, corner, fall down, stay down, stay up, don't be a coward. It's not that complicated."

Ace shook his head. "Close enough I guess." He studied Luke —soaked in sangria, chugging his bottle of the stuff, and sweating through his collar. "Another note, get cleaned up before you run. The bulls don't have great eyesight, but they'll smell you. They'd fuck you up right now, Luke, for example."

Luke raised his arms, sangria sloshing, as though a toddler asking what he did wrong.

"We'll want to seem presentable anyway if we want to get laid," Dusten remarked.

"Right, well, let's go out and see what you troglodytes can pull."

Eventually the travel and the booze became too much, and the four new arrivals had to attempt sleep. They left Ace and Hektar talking to some Norwegian girls about seeing the fireworks and headed back to the apartment. After washing the sangria and sweat off his body, Michael lay down to sleep as the party raged on outside his window. Multiple times throughout the night he woke to the blast of trumpets and drums as a musical battle waged. There was zero regard for time, he saw, whenever he checked his watch. At any moment of the night, you could walk out onto the street and be pulled into a celebration of humanity. Michael was reminded of the times he had been woken up in Afghanistan, by real rockets, and didn't sleep that well.

# CHAPTER 27

0700. MICHAEL GOT UP AND LOOKED OUT HIS WINDOW. The streets were ominously quiet in contrast to the wildness present before dawn. Washed clean of the celebration humanity had poured onto the streets, the cobblestones sat dark and damp. The sun was out, shining on parts of the buildings and casting long shadows on the ground. He turned and gave Ned's bed a kick to wake him up, then got dressed.

Ace led them through the streets to warm up their muscles, then had them duck between the wooden slats of a barricade that had been placed sometime in the morning. They had arrived on the route a full thirty minutes before the first rocket was set to launch. Michael looked around, recognizing a few faces that he had met drunkenly the night before; exchanging a grim nod and a good luck, he and the rest of the group walked to the Ayuntamiento building to claim their spots, laughing nervously as they did so.

As they waited, the police came through the crowd, leading a business-minded individual through the masses. Michael wasn't sure, but he thought they were doing a final walk-through of the route to pull out anyone too drunk before all hell broke loose. He was glad he was sober, or at least sober enough to fool the policemen, who didn't look in the mood to play anyone's games. They continued through the street, lecturing people about putting cameras away, or rounding up those too intoxicated either from early drinks or from never having ended their nights. As they passed the group a nervous energy trickled through Michael, forcing him to hop in place or kick his legs out to try to release it. It only seemed to grow as Ace led the group uphill from the start of the route to hold spots looking in the direction they'd just come, where the herd would approach from below.

The tension grew thicker, the energy all but vibrating off of the runners in the street and bouncing between the buildings. That tension rose up to fill those looking down on them from the balconies. Eyes bore down on him with a mixture of envy and concern as the minutes ticked by like hours. He was hopping in place at the spot Ace had suggested. Cheers traveled throughout the town as the town hall's bell rang out the time. Then he heard the first rocket go off.

Fear turned to focus as Ace chanted, "Hold... Hold..." The crowd on the street pushed, flowing past them, a sudden surge of the tide despite the bulls not yet having showed. Michael held his ground, doing his best to maintain his footing so he could see over those running past him and the rest of his group.

The second rocket went off.

Michael glued his eyes to the bottom of the hill; he was getting pushed along the street despite his best efforts.

Then he saw them. Like Moses parting the red sea, horns split a tidal wave of white down the middle. A scream let out from one of the balconies. Humans were shoved to either side of the street. A few brave souls committed to the center of the road. For a second, he saw the steers, their bells clinging and clanging around their necks. A primal panic poured through Michael as he saw the darker, smaller Toros Bravos—and their horns.

"*RUN!*" Ace screamed.

Michael turned and started running as fast as the crowd would let him. He tried to sprint but found himself pushed to one side or another by those surrounding him even as he tried to hold the middle. The thunder of hooves and the clanging of cowbells filled his world as he strained his neck to look over his shoulder. The lead bull entered the open space and bore down on him. Reaching a full sprint now, with most everyone else pushing to the street's edges, he veered to the side farthest from the Ayuntamiento as the bull completed the slight curve right behind him. Instinct took over and he leapt to his right, snapping his head to his left as he did so. The lead bull kept to the middle, continuing down the street alongside him. Michael kept pace with it, could see the individual strands of a white coat marbled with black, the beautifully colored streaks reminiscent of granite. Michael fought to keep up with the horned block of stone, every step lasting for minutes, knowing it would pull ahead and not wanting it to. He watched his hand as if were not his own closing the distance, his fingers extended like Adam reaching out to God. And for a microsecond, they connected.

Then it was gone, the rest of the herd appearing alongside him. Michael kept running, watching the bulls pass him over his left shoulder. Out of breath, he kept looking over his shoulder while stealing glances at the tail ends of the bulls as they blew past. He looked across the open gap the bulls had left, breathing hard yet still alert, and slowed to a walk, watching the tidal wave of human bodies close the gap, running after the herd.

It had lasted only a few seconds, but he knew already that the moments had imprinted on his soul.

He waited, studying the faces of those behind him on the route. Some still looking panicked, but most calm. Michael hadn't counted how many bulls had gone by but felt that the danger was over. He still had his head on a swivel when he spotted Hektar, smiling like a lunatic. Next to him, wearing a similar look, was Ace. Ace walked over and took one look at him. He laughed, giving Michael a small punch on the shoulder. "Do I even need to ask?"

The third rocket went off, and Michael looked back down toward where the bulls had come from. "When do we do it again?"

"Tomorrow morning and every day of fiesta if we can all keep this up."

Michael realized that his face muscles were straining from the smile on his face. It was the best he'd felt in a long time.

# CHAPTER 28

The three of them walked back down the run route, looking for the others. They found them not far off, wearing grins as they emerged from a crowd that had piled up on the outside of the turn of the street to the Ayuntamiento. They reunited just in time to move sideways as the clean-up steers cantered down the cobblestones. Ace slapped one on its rear end with an "Alright, boys, time to check the highlight reel and get a drink."

Excitement carried them down the still-barricaded route to an open side street where a television replayed the run. They all got a good laugh when it showed Dusten and Luke getting tangled up on each other and falling down. Ace had the highlight run, leading the bulls down the street while unleashing a primal scream as he ran a good fifty-foot section at the front before jumping out of the way right before the curve. "Good work, boys. Well, good try, you two. And now, it's time to watch a bunch of people get bounced around the arena by some bulls."

They pushed their way into the arena and through the still-open entrance the bulls had used. They climbed up over the walls to find a couple of open spaces so they could rest for a few moments. Soon the place was closed down with a large crowd still on the sandy floor of the arena. A gate on the far end of the arena opened and a calf with capped horns burst onto the sand. Michael got a good laugh as the beast ran through the crowd and connected pretty hard with a few out there on the ground. The group watched for a little while longer before Ace suggested it was time for a drink.

At the corner of Plaza del Castillo was an open window where a bartender was handing out the same drink to everyone in line. Ace got them all a round. Chocolate milk and cognac. Michael laughed as Ace passed the cups around and explained that it was a drink that the Basque fed unruly gringos to come down. For Michael, it was a magical potion that settled his stomach and cleared his head from the adrenaline high as well as balanced the alcohol still in his system from the night before. He took a moment while sipping to admire the healthy pours that the bartender added with a glass bottle of Yoohoo to a plastic table glass. The sight made him smile; he wouldn't have to argue about the amount of alcohol he was getting served in this country.

Drinks in hand they mingled with the crowd around the bar, almost exclusively runners. Michael shuffled around until he found himself next to Hektar, talking to a tall elderly Irishman with dark hair and green eyes. Handsome, he was all smiles, and welcomed them in like a patriarch at a family reunion.

"Good run today, lads. I saw you both on opposite sides of the herd today. Impressive work!"

"Thanks—did you run?" Michael asked.

"No, laddie, my running days are long over. Now I watch over those who do and try to give newcomers insight into what this whole fiesta is all about."

Michael took a drink. "So it's not just an adrenaline spike to cure a hangover so you can keep partying?"

He laughed. "No, my boy, it's all about the bulls, although there's an argument for your theory, and to tell you the truth I've used it for that many times." He leaned in toward both of them. "So tell me. Are you two going to the corridas tonight? The bullfights? You ran with them, you should go see what the bulls were running toward."

Michael thought about that brief moment when he had touched the lead bull and suddenly couldn't imagine not seeing the end of that story. "I think I have to see it."

Hektar nodded. "I've been curious and reading about it, so I have to see it at least once."

The man smiled and nodded at both of them, then turned to Hektar. "Hemingway?"

"I brought *Death in the Afternoon* with me on this trip and I also read *The Sun Also Rises* when I was in high school. Plus a few things I could find online."

"Excellent, that will give you an idea when you go watch, but you two might have a few questions after you witness it in person. Don't go into it thinking it's a sporting event, think of it more like a drama. Some people get it and some people don't, so if it grabs you come by the Bar Windsor on the other side of the plaza afterward. My friend and I might be able to put some things into perspective for you."

Michael finished his drink. "Sounds good."

The man smiled. "Have another drink, gentlemen, and enjoy the day. You've already proved to the world that you are alive."

Michael laughed at that. "Nothing like suicidal tendencies to start off the morning."

The smile dimmed somewhat. "All life is suicide, lad, you either kill yourself by being in the wrong place at the wrong time or you kill yourself by living too long. The trick is to be happy with whatever fate throws at you."

# CHAPTER 29

After their morning drinks they went to breakfast at a restaurant on some side street with a bunch of the other runners. They ordered eggs, pimento peppers, jamón, and caldo de toro. Michael almost believed the waiter when he told them the tail came from one of the bulls killed in the arena. Wine, water, and beer filled the table as some forty people crowded one side of the street at long tables and benches, occasionally having to rise and scoot in as a vehicle came past. Down the street Michael heard someone singing; no music, only a single voice above the chatter and clatter of the meal.

After a nap and a late lunch, the group split into two for the evening. Michael and Hektar were off to the bullfights, while Ace and the rest chose to hang out with a large group of Australians they had met at lunchtime. Michael and Hektar purchased tickets in the sol y sombra section of the arena, close to the arena floor. They also rented cushions on Ace's recommendation and brought along wine, cheese, bread, and Spanish chorizo for snacks as they took in the spectacle. The arena was gigantic, round and looking very much like the Colosseum. Taking their seats, Michael tried to absorb the full scene, from the sand of the arena floor to the crowds packed into the cheap spots high above.

Over his shoulder, he noticed the viewing boxes for the VIPs. In the central one sat those Michael assumed presided over the arena, each like a modern-day Caesar, looking down at the sands below them, passing judgement.

Across the arena, revelers in the sunny section sprayed sangria and tossed items back and forth like this was a party at the beach. Right in the middle of them was a brass band, playing for the crowd.

"What's with the guys in the front row sitting with their backs to the arena?" Michael asked when he saw them.

Hektar looked to where he was pointing. "I don't know. Could be a form of protest?"

"What, like PETA?"

"I don't know. They do protest the fiesta every year before the start."

Michael looked at the broad backs. "They don't look like PETA."

Hektar shrugged. "Who knows, then. Guess not every Spaniard is a fan of this tradition."

Michael thought about his argument with Heide about the bullfight, but it hadn't occurred to him that there might be those in Spain who wouldn't be fans. He shrugged it off and turned his attention back to the center as it exploded with adulation. The three matadors and their retinue, brightly colored in different flashing suits of lights, entered the arena.

The lead matador wore green and gold, vaguely reminding Michael of the fatigues he wore in Afghanistan, albeit with the opposite effect. His entourage followed, similarly but less extravagantly dressed, all moving to the middle of the arena to the sounds of trumpets.

Peering over his seat, "Is the matador wearing an eyepatch?" Michael asked.

"Yeah, I heard that he was gored through the face and lost an eye."

"Looks like a pirate with that hat. And he's still doing it?"

"I think that's his nickname name now. La Pirata. Saw him running on the streets with us this morning."

"That's a whole different breed of human right there." Michael wondered what would drive a man to run in the morning, then get into a showdown with that animal in the afternoon. Then he wondered what had driven him to go to war, then come here to run. Maybe it was encoded in his DNA or maybe it was some thread of fate. As he watched the ceremony, he raised his wine in respect.

They watched as the matador and his men saluted the president of the arena above them. Once acknowledged by the president, they retreated behind the narrow openings along the low wall surrounding the arena. The matador wearing the eye patch came out to the center of the arena, brandishing a heavy, bicolored cape—the dull yellow-gold nearest him and the magenta facing out. For a moment the audience grew quiet as the matador stepped toward a red gate. Michael watched as La Pirata's shoulders heaved with heavy breaths. He dropped to his knees in front of the door and crossed himself several times, seemingly muttering a prayer while he knelt. Then he made a gesture. The attendant nodded at him and pulled the gate open, revealing nothing but darkness on the inside.

The bull exploded out of the shadows and into the light. Finding the kneeling figure it lowered its horns and charged. As the bull drew near, the matador brought the cape in front of him. Moved it to his right in the split-second it took for the bull to cover the ground. The bull leapt through the cape, centimeters from the matador's shoulder. It soared through the empty air. The matador got to his feet as its tail whipped by his face. The man turned to face the bull. The bull landed and turned, facing the man, charging again. La Pirata ran backward a few feet, gaining some distance from the horns, then with another wave of the cape, passed the bull harmlessly to one side. Like a pirate captain uses sails to harness the energy of the wind to maneuver his ship, the matador synched more and more passes with the bull, fueled by every rush of air from its charges. "*Olé!*" screamed the crowd on each successful pass.

The matador, Michael realized, had lured the bull toward the opposite side of the arena from the gate. Two riders entered on horses wearing padded armor and blinders. Each man carried a long spear with a bar bisecting the shaft about six inches from the point.

"What's this about?" he asked, nudging Hektar.

"Picadors. They allow the bull to charge the horse, tiring him out and taking the opportunity to pierce its neck and weaken the muscle. They want the bull to move with its head down in the final stage of the fight."

"Why's that?"

"The matador must jump over the bull's horns to drive a sword between the upper ribs. If the head isn't low enough, he can't place the sword in the right position to sever the aorta and grant the bull a quick death."

Michael nodded. "I'm surprised the horses don't get torn apart. That armor doesn't look like much."

Hektar looked at the horses. "From what I've read, they used to not receive armor at all. Dozens of horses would be sacrificed in the arena to wear out a bull."

The bull was busy lifting a horse off its feet while a picador stabbed at its heavily muscled neck. Blood poured through the wound at a steady trickle, down the marbled coat. It was then that Michael registered that this was the bull he had run with this morning, touching the creature as they both barreled down the streets of Pamplona together. The moment replayed, that brief second that had lasted forever.

The memory of contact kept his full attention on the spectacle in front of him, his entire focus the bull. The cheers of the crowd diminished, the notes played by the band faded. Hektar said something he didn't comprehend as the bull followed the matador. He watched as the bull disregarded the damage from the spearmen to lift horse and rider again. He couldn't take his eyes off the blood dripping out of the wounds. His hand slid to his own neck, aching fiercely for the first time since arriving in Spain.

The hazy tune from the band shifted as the horses left the arena. The bull, alone now, huffed its panic, chest expanding violently as air filled its lungs, head turning to see who dared challenge it next, standing tall as it took the center. Dark red rolled down its coat as the one-eyed matador returned, brandishing long pinata-esque sticks with barbed, bladed ends. The crowd went berserk as the matador advanced to the center of the arena.

Hektar leaned into Michael. "Usually, the matador has one of his cuadrilla put those in for him."

The matador faced the bull with a barb in each hand; holding them out above his head, ends pointed down and away from him, he lowered his stance in challenge. The bull accepted and charged. The matador, arms still raised, shuffled forward two paces toward the oncoming animal. Mere steps from the creature, he jumped. Jabbed the points into the neck of the bull. Landing clear of the animal, he backpedaled.

Outraged, the bull chuffed and pawed the ground. His ground. The matador ran back to the outer arena and produced two more barbs. Hands with harpoons aloft again, he squared off with the bull once more, pushed close, and with a loud "*Ha!*" and a jump, enticed the bull into racing at him again. He moved in with the barbs, jumped sideways to avoid the horns. Swung. Danced away like an acrobat. The barb stuck up in the bull's hide within an inch of the one already placed.

Hektar again said something to Michael, but all he heard was "banderilla," too in tune with the movements of the bull to comprehend the rest.

With what Michael now assumed were the banderillas in place, the matador gestured to the president of the arena. A flourish from the band sounded, then La Pirata produced a small, blood-red cape and a ruby-handled sword from behind the low wall. He tossed his black cap in defiance into the middle of the arena. It landed right side up. He approached the bull, who had staked a claim to ground closer to the arena door where he'd entered. As he inched closer, the matador gave a flick of his wrist, and the bull sped through the red, both actors turning and moving as one in a sequence that brought more "*OLÉs!*" from the crowd. The matador fixed himself to position, an axle to turn the bull with a wave of the cape, a stomp of his foot, a challenge of "*Toro! Eh!*" The frustration and determination, the exhaustion and the desperation of the animal soared, too, in Michael as it kept attacking and failing to conquer its enemy. There was no quit as it fought this intruder in the space that it had claimed as his own.

A pass caused the bull to stumble in a full turn and stop in its tracks, breathing heavily as the matador turned his back to it and embraced the cheers from the crowd. The bull's head lowered. The matador faced it once more and crept forward, cape lowered to the level of the bull's eyes as he sighted down the shaft of the sword as though it were a gun barrel. All those passes, and an unstoppable force now looked stoppable, its energy drained to turn the impossible possible.

Michael had expected to find controlled anger on the face of the matador as on one in a fight. Instead, he found a grim resignation as on one in mourning. Such passion and empathy from a man about to kill knocked Michael off guard. A chemistry of intimacy between man and beast crackled. Tears fell from the matador's lone eye; the animal's eyes teared as well.

The man moved precisely, determined in his task. A single movement. A flash of the cape in front of the bull. The bull surging forward. The matador leaping, extending his frame over the horns. And driving the sword down to the hilt in a spot just below the neck.

The matador pivoted away, letting the cape fall from his hands as the bull took it in its horns. Arms outstretched like Christ crucified, the matador backed away, attention fixed on the bull.

The bull surged in search for its target, blood spilling from its mouth and nostrils. A heartbeat. It fell to its knees. Another pulse on its side, defiant to the end. Dead.

The crowd rose to its feet in unison, screaming and applauding. Hektar stood up along with them. Michael looked at the bull, then to the faces around him. He saw grown men and women with tears in their eyes, all caught in the artistry of the moment. The matador took a lap around the arena. He looked back at the bull, who was now being hooked up to a horse-drawn cart, getting dragged out of the arena. Then Michael stood up as he watched the bull leave a broad indentation in the sand.

He touched his face. Wet.

He couldn't remember the last time he cried.

# CHAPTER 30

Five more bulls, five more deaths. Hektar and Michael moved from the arena into the streets as night fell on the city. Shoulders knocked as they pushed through the never-ending bodies dressed in white and red to reach Plaza del Castillo. They crossed it and came to the Bar Windsor, and found the man they met earlier seated with a balding gentleman with a hawkish face framed by a set of sideburns befitting a Victorian Cavalry officer. At the sight of them, the Irishman gestured to them to take a seat at the table.

"So, lads, you've had your first encierro and your first corrida. What do you think?"

Michael sat down. "I'm still wrapping my head around what I saw." He remembered the first bull, from his morning contact with it to its death in the afternoon. "I'm not sure how I feel about it."

"That's fair," the hawkish man said with a Welsh accent. "Just remember one thing, this belongs to the Spanish, so any moral qualms you have about the bulls aren't yours to spread."

He waved a comely waitress over for drinks to be delivered to the table.

His companion from Ireland smiled coolly. "I think the main thing you have to come to terms with is deciding who you identified with when you watched the corrida. Where you simply part of the crowd, observing a spectacle? Did you focus on the matador, in awe of his bravery? Or were you in the *arena*? Looking at life from behind a set of horns?"

Michael took a breath. "That."

Hektar nodded along in agreement with him.

"Good," the Irishman continued, smile unfaltering. "You know, then, that you're watching an artist create a tragedy of life and death."

"It is akin to ritual sacrifice, something holy that demands respect," the hawkish man offered. "It's not simple entertainment."

Nodding to his friend's insight, the Irishman said, "That it is. You're not viewing sport, but something ancient and primal."

Michael thought back to when he was in the arena. "Some people in the crowd—Spaniards—they had their backs turned to the fight the whole time. Is this not disrespectful?"

The Irishman smiled still. "You see, Spain has a"—he opened his hands—"complicated past. This region here is Basque—I myself am Basque, though my family left to the United Kingdom during the Spanish Civil War. That war's divisions persist today." He looked at the both of them. "Your American Civil War left scars and unhealed wounds, yes? It is the same here. There are those who view the corrida as a Nationalist symbol forced upon us by the dictatorship of Francisco Franco. The moral and ethical qualms, they exist too."

The hawkish man spat to his side, then leaned in. "They have no legitimate reason to disrespect the animal or the matador doing his job."

"You have to forgive my friend, an aficionado to his core. He takes it as his role in life to defend the corrida."

"Apologies if I'm seeming rude." The man sat back in his chair. "Lies and misinformation spread such that I can't help but defend the bulls and explain what is actually happening both inside the ring and outside it." The server came to the table with a tray of beverages, and the hawkish man passed beers around and paid the server. "Everything that happens in the arena has a purpose. All so that a man on foot can kill via a single blow with a sword. It is the last true gladiatorial spectacle humanity has to offer. Drawing out emotion with the drama of a live performance so that one can witness beauty even in death."

Michael paused at those words. "Then the bull always dies?"

"Oh, there are times when a bull is deemed extraordinary by the matador, by the crowd, and the people appeal for the bull to be pardoned. It is rare, and a great honor for the matador." The hawkish man frowned. "The crowd in Pamplona, however, tends to agitate the bull beyond the matador's control, and so he'll never draw out the best of what the animal has to offer. That's the matador's job, you see. To demonstrate the nobility, the bravery, of the bull in the arena. As it charges, he is charged with bringing each pass closer to taking his life, bringing the audience into the moment. Here, the taunts from an inebriated crowd of tourists?" He spat again. "In other arenas, it's like stepping into a church. Unfortunately, Pamplona is usually a traveler's first and only introduction to the corrida. If you want any hope of witnessing a pardon, you'll have to become a true aficionado and attend the ferias and corridas across Spain. In Andalucía, in Seville, por ejemplo, the corrida is most sacred."

"A pardoned bull." Michael shook his head. "It is set free?"

"It is returned to the ranch where it originated and becomes a seed bull."

"Breeding the next generation of fighting bulls," the Irishman added. "Take for instance the bulls from today. Had one been pardoned it would return to the pastures of Fuente Ymbro. To live its life out on open pastures, a marvelous creature allowed to roam on land that is protected by the Spanish government."

"They're treated, then? The wounds to the neck?" Michael asked, his own neck burning as if echoing the suffering of the six bulls.

"Up until the sword is driven in, everything is superficial. Even the banderillas, the barbed sticks, which act mainly as a way of correcting the bull and giving it a jolt. But yes, veterinarians clean and stitch the wounds."

Michael leaned back. "So the bull is fighting for its freedom."

The hawkish man snorted. "Americans. The bull fights because it is a fighting bull. You two, you have served in the military. I can tell. Did you fight for your freedom? Why did you not stay among the others who shied away from conflict, living lives of quiet desperation?"

Michael and Hektar shared a look.

"You chose a life of fighting, of service. Called to something other than domestication back in the colonies. Compare the fighting bull's life to that of one bred for meat. A meat cow is culled at two years, the fighting bull sent to the arena at four.

Who gets the better quality of life? The one roaming the plains or the one kept in the safety and security of the farm? One bred to entertain your soul, the other to entertain your palate." He leaned in. "It makes you wonder what type of life you're living."

Silence. That memory, back again. The weight of that incredible moment, brushing fingers against life mere hours before its death.

The Irishman smoothed out his friend's statements. "That's why we go to the corridas, why we once ran. Why we can spot those in the crowd who appreciate the art, the life the Toro Bravo lives. Why, when we are gifted a listening ear, we offer some education on the matter." He grinned as he straightened. "It should give you more to think about when you run with them again."

Michael and Hektar left the gentlemen at the bar and met with the rest of the group back at the apartment. They shared what they had seen and learned. Ace seemed unimpressed.

"I'm just here for the run. I've already seen what happens in the arena."

The rest of the group decided, almost offhandedly, that they'd go tomorrow evening, willing to let Hektar take them along. They had a few more drinks at the apartment, then headed back onto the streets to go view the fireworks with the group of Australians that Ace had partied with earlier.

The groups swapped stories and cultural eccentricities as they walked to an open field outside of the older part of Pamplona near the bus station. They found some real estate and settled back and watched a fireworks display that rivaled any Fourth of July celebration Michael had ever seen. As he watched, he was reminded of the different firefights he'd survived. Days of heavy adrenaline rushes in Afghanistan, incoming and outgoing tracers streaming across the darkness. A similar scene contrasted only by one's seriousness and the other's lightheartedness. Maybe this was how combat was conducted in ancient times. Battle waged in the morning, victory celebrated at night. But in that context, wouldn't the bull be his enemy?

The more he thought about that, the more he understood the emotion he saw on the matador's face as he killed.

# CHAPTER 31

0700. THE WATCH VIBRATED MICHAEL AWAKE. THE RITUAL they had developed—kicking Ned out of bed, having coffee with everyone, exchanging glum looks in the apartment—started over. Now that they knew what to expect, their anxiety hit as soon as they ventured out onto the streets into the warm sun. Ace led them to the wooden fence that barricaded the run route. Those they recognized returned their handshakes, wishing good luck, the occasional "Suerte." Their spot waited on the top of Santo Domingo.

On the way up, Michael saw a small statue being paraded down the street, held delicately by one man. Individuals kissed the effigy as it continued down Santo Domingo. On an impulse, Michael turned from the group and followed it down the walled street to the start of the run near where the bulls were paddocked. Runners parted and paid their respects as the idol traveled past them. Finally, it came to a notch in a stone wall. A ladder appeared, reaching up to the empty shelf, and the man lifted Saint Fermin into its place. A crowd gathered and, together, began chanting.

"A San Fermín pedimos, por ser nuestro patrón, no guíe en el encierro dándonos sus bendición!"

A warmth fluttered above Michael's navel and spread to his heart, filling him with an energy and vibrance that he had never felt before. The idol—one hand pointed to the sky, the Shepard's crook raised in the other—looked down on him as though the source of this newfound energy within him.

Michael shook his head, smiled to himself, and moved back up the street. He found Ace and the others waiting where he'd left them. As he walked up, Ace grabbed him. "You running with us? Now that you have an idea of what's in store?"

"I'm not sure. This spot was fun yesterday."

Ace smiled. "Here's a move for you. Look up at the balconies, find a little hottie you want to impress, and run in front of her. Works like a charm, if you can find her." His smile dropped. "Just try not to do anything stupid."

"Like getting gored?"

"Like getting gored."

"Could go for the sympathy play, couldn't I?"

"That only works if you have her name and she's actually interested in you and you live. The only visitors you'll have in the hospital will be our ugly mugs, sweating booze all over you and telling you you're an idiot. And then we'll leave you there to go back to the party while you watch from a hospital bed."

Michael peered at the balconies out of the corner of his eye. "Good to know I can't ruin this for ya'll." He tilted back his head to properly see all the women watching the event, but the aching above his spine caused him to bring his head back down. He walked down the street, past the Ayuntamiento and toward the start of the curve, and looked up once more; a jolt brought his head back down. He looked at the curve, at the photographers above the barricade already snapping pictures, at the camera operator lazily pointing his lens at the sky. All of them waiting for something to happen.

Michael looked at the cameras, Ace's advice coming to mind. He wasn't here to get anyone's attention. He wanted to run with the bulls. He was here for himself. What better way to do this than in the most difficult spot? He looked at the painting of San Fermín on the opposite side of the street and knew this was where he was meant to be. "Okay, here's my spot," Michael said to himself, looking behind him and then at the street before him. The curve. This was the route he'd take.

He took stock of those around him. A bunch of Spaniards warming up, saying their prayers. A very large German man Michael met the night before but whose name he couldn't remember. He nodded to him and received a nod in return. The tension as the time went by spun inside him, his face contorting from grimace to pleasure and back as all the possibilities of what could happen came to mind. Staring at the curve, he debated whether he should take La Curva's inside or run on the outside. He couldn't remember what Ace had told him about this spot on the run route other than don't try it. He decided to use the ninety-degree turn to his advantage by cutting straight across as though forming a triangle. That settled, he repositioned himself, picking a spot that would in his estimation, allow him to reach a full sprint.

The first rocket went off. The balconies above erupted with cheers and the people on the street surged with anticipation.

He bounced and tried to maintain the area he'd claimed, to stay on his feet. He resisted the crowds moving around him, holding the center as he was pushed toward the outside by the bodies shoving past. Michael held his own, then *BOOM!* The second rocket.

Fear and anticipation abandoned him; he was in the moment. He strained to keep his eyes up to see the herd. He heard them before he saw them, hooves striking cobblestones, cowbells ringing in unison. He turned to run but was blocked by the crowd and forced to jog. He looked over his shoulder and the lead bulls tore into the curve. All he could do was get out of the way as they thundered past him. Wanting, needing, to be part of the herd, he shoved back into the center and chased after them into the turn, checking over his shoulder as he did to see if any more bulls were coming.

His shin hit something hard, like concrete, and he was flying through the air, diving forward, hands outstretched. Before him, a blur of a dark coat—a bull that had lost its footing and fallen in front of him having failed to complete the turn. Michael landed on his belly next to the downed bull. It chuffed and flailed, fighting to get to its feet. Michael, prone, inched his way away from the bull as it gained purchase on the cobblestones. He could smell the pasture, grass and manure, along with musk. Could feel its breath on him as it found its footing. Michael gazed in awe at the horned figure towering above him.

With a snort, it ignored Michael where he lay defenseless on the ground and instead charged a group of people who had gathered a few paces in front of them. Michael saw his huge German friend among them and watched as the bull hit the man and casually flipped him over its horns. It ran through the rest of them, sending grown men into the air like struck bowling pins. Someone leaped over Michael, a man in a green polo wielding a long wooden stick in one hand. El pastor sprinted after the bull, smacking it on its hindquarters as it pressed an unlucky human into the wall. The bull turned from its work on the runner. Another smack, and it took off down the street, chasing after the rest of the herd.

Michael muttered a prayer to himself and a thank you to his green-shirted savior as he lay there. Then hands lifted him off the ground and his feet settled under him, ready to run. He looked back toward the beginning of the curve but saw no bulls coming. The third rocket went off as he wondered if he had made a fool out of himself.

# CHAPTER 32

"So when you told us over and over not to do anything stupid, is this what you were talking about?" Dusten asked, looking at the television screen that was replaying the footage of Michael flying over the bull again and again.

Ace shook his head at Michael. "At least you had the good sense to stay down. I told you to avoid the curve. What in hell made you want to try it?"

Michael shrugged. "Why try to get one girl's attention when you can get everyone's?"

Ace just stared at him for a moment. "Chicks dig scars and you did stand out from the crowd. But not in a good way. Maybe take a look around and run another area. There are cameras everywhere."

"Maybe I did it for myself too."

Ace laughed. "Hopefully you got that out of your system, then."

Michael nodded his head to Ace and thought, *Not likely*. He watched the replay one more time, wishing he had gotten it right.

"You'll get a chance to redeem yourself, but from the looks of it you spent all your luck on the street this morning."

Michael continued to nod.

Dusten snorted. "Have another drink, Doc. I'm sure your next run will be just fine."

"Look on the bright side," Ned said, pointing at the television. "Everyone in the city is going to recognize you."

Ace shook his head as he, too, rewatched the run. "You'll be famous for a day at least. Alright, boys, let's go get that post-run drink," he said, leading them around to the corner bar for a chocolate milk and cognac.

Ned was right. Michael did find himself the center of attention. Everyone from the bartender to the people standing in line recognized his run, many asking him about it. Ace grumbled to himself as Michael stole all the attention yet happily accepted a free drink from the bruised German who was chatting with Michael about their encounter that morning.

On his second beverage and fifth retelling of the story, Michael noticed the most beautiful woman he'd ever seen across the plaza. Statuesque with an hourglass figure, smiling and laughing, causally surrounded by male admirers. Her brown eyes caught Michael's and she held his gaze, the look bewitching. She excused herself and strode over to him, sunlight catching her long curly brown hair and turning it red for a moment.

Michael's feet carried him to meet her halfway. "You were the one on the corner this morning, under our balcony, weren't you?" A North American accent he couldn't place.

Michael chuckled. "Probably me."

She put her hands on her hips, head tilted inquisitively, a slight smirk on her face. "I don't understand you men, why you feel the need to participate in an idiotic tradition that could possibly kill you."

"Why were you watching it if you feel that way?"

"I enjoy watching men do stupid things. Makes me feel superior." She had a confident flirtatious quality to her tone that Michael loved. "Tell me, why were you out there?"

"If I knew the answer to that maybe I wouldn't feel the need to do stupid things."

She cocked her head, eyes sparkling "I think you know. Maybe you simply can't admit it."

"Do you usually interrogate people before you introduce yourself?"

She smiled. "Only the ones I think deserve it. Let me guess, this is your first time at fiesta?"

Michael nodded. "This place, it's... intense."

"It is, but it's so much fun. I've been lucky that my family has gotten to come here a couple of times. The party is nonstop and more amped up than anywhere else I've been in the world."

"You don't come for the bulls at all, then?"

The hands on her hips balled into fists. "I respect the bulls, but I'm here to enjoy my life, not see an animal lose theirs. If I had it my way, we'd all just enjoy the fiesta, the good friends and drinks, the laughing and dancing and singing." That bewitching look came back to her face. "You know—love life. You don't need the run or the fight for any of that."

"Don't you think that's part of what adds to the intensity? I mean, without the death and tragedy, something would be taken away."

"There's always more to it than just a party, even without the bulls." She said with a sly smile. "It's about family, love, celebration. I get the sense that you're not understanding that part."

"Maybe I'm just not used to having those things in my life."

"Everyone has those things in life if they look for them."

Michael let out a slight laugh. "Well, I might be cursed with needing an adrenaline fix to make up for being blind to those things."

"And is that all you want out of life?" She studied him closely. "An adrenaline fix?"

Michael's eyes unfocused. "I don't know. To tell you the truth, this is the best I've felt in a long time." His focus came back to her. "I'd need a great reason to give that all away."

She laughed at him. "You're like all the rest. You'll keep coming back to the streets year after year trying to prove to yourself or maybe to everyone else that you can. So I think the real question is: Who do you want to be?"

"What do you mean by that?"

"If this is the best you've ever felt, then is this what you're going to dedicate your life to?"

Michael thought about that question. "This was a bucket list type of thing." He looked over his shoulder back at his brothers who were still in the service. "I'm not sure what to I want to dedicate my life to now."

"Don't you think you should figure that out?"

Crossing his arms. "I'm currently in the forget about the past, live in the present mood."

Her playful smile turned into a frown, her own arms folding. "That's a good start, but you should really figure that out. Then ask yourself if you are willing to sacrifice who you are to be become who you want to be. Until then, you'll miss out on all the life around you while you focus on that silly run."

"Oh, and what life is that?"

The smirk and playfulness returned to her face. "When you figure that out come find me." With that, she turned and sashayed away from him.

"Wait! I'm Michael. What's your name?"

She turned and smiled at him. "I'm Grace, Michael." Then she walked away, leaving Michael to contemplate both his empty glass and the empty space she once held.

# CHAPTER 33

After a necessary nap, Michael met up with Ace, and Hektar took the other three to the corridas. The two went out barhopping, but Michael couldn't get Grace off his mind. Ace would keep pulling him back into another English-speaking group, they'd have a few drinks with them, and the two would meander off to another spot. Hours later, they walked into a bar close to the arena called La Mafia, and Ace passed Michael a beer.

"Are you good, bud? You seem distracted. Party's not getting to ya now, is it?"

"Just got someone on my mind."

"One? I've introduced you to over a dozen gorgeous honeys from all over the globe."

"Have you ever thought about settling down with just one? Or is this all you need?"

Ace smiled, scanning the crowded room filled with white and flashes of red, then looked directly at Michael. "I'm always going to need more. That's why I do what I do. I don't know how to relax. I've tried it back in the States, and I always fuck it up. Settling down? Starting a family? That's not the type of guy I am." He grew forlorn. "Wasn't the type of guy Conchord was either." He held Michael's eye. "Look, I don't know that I can give you the right answer. I come here, and I enjoy myself. I bring others here so they can enjoy them-selves. My advice? Quit looking for answers and just have fun. There are too many like us who didn't get to make it home. Who didn't get the chance to do shit like this. I'm doing my best to live it up for all the assholes out there like Conchord. Or Porter, poor bastard, stuck at home with a wife and a baby on the way. Could have been living it up with us but noooo. He had to go and breed." Ace chuckled into his glass.

Michael looked at all the strangers around them. "Yeah, poor bastard." He bought Ace a drink and slipped out as Ace slid into yet another group of female tourists. His feet led him into the streets, where he searched for Grace. At every party and bar he pushed into, he'd catch a glimpse of curly hair, flashing red in the lights, luring him like a matador's cape. Every time, he'd give chase, only to find it belonged to another person. He eventually headed down to the fair-grounds. Here, not all that distant from the hard-partying revelers, families enjoyed nighttime picnics, played games, rode carnival rides, conversed about life. It was a whole other side of fiesta—one he felt barred from experiencing. He was about to turn away from the fairgrounds with its family festivities when he saw her. Grace. All smiles as she walked through the fair arm-in-arm with a slightly younger and lighter-haired version of herself. Behind them walked an older couple from whom the two beauties must have originated.

As Michael watched them, more of their siblings—shared blood clear from their faces, from their way of fluttering close to each other—appeared, every one of them laughing, joking, living in the moment. Living for this time together. The father tightened his loving embrace with his wife, the two of them standing back, faces aglow with pride and satisfaction, and watching their grown children enjoy being alive.

Michael stayed out of sight, envious. Envious of this man who'd created this picturesque life. He suddenly missed Porter.

He let Grace and her family pass. He wanted to pursue them, wanted them to bring him into their fold. The sangria in his hand, deep in its ruby hue, reflected back his broken home and pursuits. Such a life, it wasn't for him. He hadn't earned that yet.

He finished his drink and went back toward the center of town in pursuit of a refill. It was well past midnight and the Bar Windsor was still crowded, but he managed to spot the two older gentlemen from the other night sitting in the same spot with a lone chair in front of them. They waved him over.

"You look like you're searching," the Irishman said.

Michael chuckled. "For another drink." He looked back in the direction of the fairgrounds. "And a girl I met this morning after the run. Haven't been able to get her out of my head."

The hawkish man sat back and studied Michael. His eyes fell on the bracelet he wore. "You're a warrior and a bull runner; she should be pursuing you."

His companion laughed and gave his friend a friendly tap on the shoulder. "You know as well as I do that when a young man gets a beauty in his heart there's no sense. Especially for a warrior and a bull runner. A hard lesson for us all." Taking a sip of his cocktail. "He'll have to learn as we did about bulls and women and war. All have a tendency to bring a man to his knees." He cupped his drink, wearing that smile that never left his face. "Some women have this magical quality that brings to the surface every pain you have buried, that has you imagining a life you never believed possible. Then they up and leave, and you're left trying to calm the ghosts of your past on your own." He looked around the plaza. "In this town, we live with our ghosts, quieting them with bulls and drinks."

"So, what? I'm supposed to keep running and drinking? That's the answer?"

The other man shook his sideburns and snorted. "Answer? There is no answer. There is only life. Away from here, you can go to work every day. Start a family. A part of you will itch to come back to the streets always. Back to the adrenaline-fueled moments when the rockets ignite. Back to living despite your fear and doubts about what's to come, just as you did in wartime. The bulls, the way they force us to run, they're here to remind us of who we really are." He took a long drink. "Those who survive."

The Irishman's smile settled to a smirk as he examined the depths of his drink. "Men like us, we wage war with ourselves. We rage against the world, it wins. We rage against ourselves, it consumes us. You can look for a woman to save you, a woman with whom you can settle down, but you will find your mind wandering back to the days when you were a soldier, wandering back to your days running on these streets. Look inside yourself, lad, and quit the rage." He looked up from the drink, cocked his head. "Or maybe not." The smile returned. "We found our peace in the streets, in our recognition of our natures within the corrida. In knowing we are bulls amongst men." He finished his drink in one long pull and set it down on the table.

The Welsh man squinted into the distance, as though seeing the bullring. "We'd risk domestication otherwise."

Silence fell on the table, the fiesta carrying on around them, suddenly so loud any more discussion seemed impossible. Michael accepted this and stood to leave, thanking both men.

The green-eyed man nodded. "Suerte, amigo."

The Hawkish man tilted his glass in a salute.

Back in the plaza, Michael released a sigh as he took in the masses of people partying without a care. He was tired, but a part of him wanted to continue his search and another part of him wanted to join in with the dancing and laughter all around him. He realized he should have at least bought the men a drink as thanks, however weak, for all their advice.

Instead he walked back to his bed on Aldapa.

As he lay down, he knew he would find no sleep tonight. He tossed and turned, waking often to the partying outside his window that never stopped, the noise coming in waves. Annoyingly, Ned slept peacefully in the bed across from him, still in possession of that infantryman's magical ability to sleep anywhere, anytime, and through anything. Michael's neck ached more than usual and he checked his watch only to be disappointed every time at the speed of the thing. Eyes on the ceiling, he wished he were somewhere else, somewhere outside of this chaos. As he wasted the night staring at the ceiling and rolling over to stare at the wall, as the horns and drums warred outside his window, he wished for quiet. The constant hum of a thousand voices rumbled on as he begged for sleep.

Maybe he should take a day off. Go outside the city and find somewhere peaceful. He could go north to San Sebastian, to its rumored beautiful beach and amazing food. He imagined Grace going with him, a day spent sunning on the sand and wading into the ocean to cool off in turn. Imagined an evening spent exploring the city. Eating, drinking, relaxing. Would he fuck it up like Ace? Somewhere a bottle rocket went off, snapping him out of his fantasy.

Finally, dawn crept through the window. As the sun grew in the sky, casting shadows on the streets below, the noise and festivities retracted from the light. Michael listened as the fiesta faded, the sounds outside his window shifting to clean-up crews and those few stubborn partiers fighting off sleep. The *thunk* of the barriers going up for the run route filtered through and he debated once more taking the morning off from the run, all these days of drinking and adrenaline, he concluded, getting to him.

He had decided to do exactly that when the watch on his wrist vibrated. The bells outside tolled. Sitting up, he looked over at Ned. Sound asleep. He got to his feet. Dressed. Gave Ned's bed a kick. Went into the kitchen.

If his guys were on the street, his place was with them. He would not abandon them.

# CHAPTER 34

AFTER DUCKING UNDER THE WOODEN BARRIERS, THEY WERE all back on the run route. Michael ignored the pressure in his neck, telling himself that after the run today he would find a peaceful place and rest in San Sebastion. Looking at the group, he debated telling them his plan.

"Miuras," Ace said as he looked at a Spanish newspaper, pulling Michael's attention back to the moment. "They're legends. Faster, stronger, and more cunning. This isn't the breed to mess around with." He gave Michael a look. "So let's not do any repeats of yesterday."

Michael smirked, rubbing the back of his neck. "No promises." He looked at the wooden barriers and thought about stepping out. Then he looked back at his brothers and pushed that idea away. He tried walking off the tension. At the start of the route, the barricade reminded him that there was no escape here. He had pushed through tougher times than this. Been more sleep deprived, more beat down. He knew he could handle it. He stopped down there at the start and waited.

Just as it had yesterday, the idol of Saint Fermin came and was put into its nook on the wall. He stood behind the men and listened, arms folded, to the benediction they chanted, watched them thrust their newspapers in time toward the idol. That surge of energy didn't come as it had the previous day. The idol stared at him, judged him, as if there was some question he was supposed to answer.

Michael followed the hill back to his group, keeping his eyes straight ahead and ignoring any side street that might offer him escape.

Ace frowned when he came into view, looking down in the direction of Saint Fermin, then at Michael. "You getting superstitious on me, my pagan brother?"

"A little stitious maybe."

"Can't hurt. Well, unless you're a heathen. Where are you running today? And don't say the curve."

"I'm going to give it another shot." The words rolled out of his mouth, taking him by surprise, all his debates about stepping out of the run a conscious reaction shoved down by his subconscious needs. Grace came to mind unbidden. She had spotted him there yesterday. If she watched today, the curve was where she'd be. The thought lifted him, took away the pain for a moment.

Ace shook his head. "I'm not going to stop you from being dumb. You do you if you must. But the rest of us are going up to the top, to help bring them into the arena. Why not join us instead of being an idiot?"

Michael deliberated for a bit. "I'm doing the curve today."

Hektar looked at Ace, then at Michael. "I'll run it with you, Doc."

Ned shrugged. "I'll run it. It'll give me a chance to kick you up when one of those bulls knocks you on your ass."

"Payback for my wake-up calls?"

"And all the years of covering your dumb ass."

Dusten looked at Luke. "We'll run it. Save the tunnel for another day."

Luke looked back at Dusten. "We will?"

"Yeah, we will. Don't you want a front row seat for whatever dumb shit Doc pulls today?"

Luke grins. "I would've loved to see yesterday's performance live."

"This is stupid," Ace said. "I've literally told all of you multiple times that you shouldn't run there, and this is what you all want to do." He pointed a finger at Michael. "Just because you can't seem to score, you feel the need to do something drastic."

Michael ignored the jab. "We're all out here anyway. Might as well take it to the limit."

Ace sighed. "Fuck it. I'll come. But if this turns out bad, don't be surprised to see me standing over you in a hospital bed saying I told you so."

"It'll be a nice change of pace from stitching you up saying I told you so."

"Fuck you, Doc." Ace looked at his watch. "Better move."

They moved down as a group past the Ayuntamiento, stopping in front of the Burger King. From there they spread out. He checked his watch; only a minute to go. He let his eyes drift to the skyline. There, high in the clear sky, hung a sliver of the moon. Waning crescent in a lopsided smile. He tried scanning the balconies, but his neck forced him to bring his eyes down.

Around him, runners said prayers or bounced to control nerves or stood stoic in the street, these last few minutes the longest for everyone. At the curve, the painting of Saint Fermin on the outside wall returned his gaze. Then all anxiety left him, everything falling into place as though he was exactly where he was supposed to be. All he had to do was complete this run. A smile creased his face as the bells began to toll.

The rocket exploded. Cheers erupted. Swarms of people streamed past him. Panicked faces a blur, calm ones steady. Michael held his ground. The second rocket sounded. The stream became a river as more bodies poured down the route. Cowbells and hooves grew louder, blending with screams from above and below. The stream now a tide, the ground vibrated under Michael. And the bulls broke through the crowd.

He turned to run, keeping to the inside, Saint Fermin his witness. A flash of pain shot through his neck as he tried to look over his shoulder to gauge the bulls' distance. He ignored it and kept running.

Almost to the middle of La Curva, the bulls nearly upon him. People had amassed along the inside of the turn, faces frozen in fear, forcing Michael closer to the center of the turn. He looked over his shoulder again and saw a black-horned blur coming right at him. His head and torso twisted to keep an eye on the bull. Hands slammed his back. Feet tangling together, he spun, facing the bull in full. He was falling back-ward, eyes to the oncoming herd, the black bull's lowered head at eye level, its horns swaying side to side. Then pressure hit him in the chest. Meat met horn, and he was no longer falling but thrown.

The bull was gone, barely having broken its stride. Michael was on his back, knowing he needed to stay down. He brought one hand to his chest, to the warmth and dampness there, pumping in time to the second hand of his watch. Crimson liquid flowed down his hand as he examined it, leaking onto the memorial bracelet he wore. He looked up at the balconies, at the horrified faces looking down at him. Michael looked around at those running by and hoped that the other guys weren't harmed. Then he turned his head back to the balconies to keep scanning above him, looking, looking for Grace.

# PART SIX
# POBRE DE MI

*"The real reason for not committing suicide is because you always
know how swell life gets again after the hell is over."*
—Ernest Hemingway

# CHAPTER 35

It was almost midnight as she wandered the streets. People crowded around each other, all holding candles as the festive mood turned somber and sober. It was the fourteenth of July, and Fiesta neared its end. Walking out of Plaza del Castillo down to the Ayuntiemento, where only a week before Fiesta had exploded into existence, now brought the revelers back to reality. Pañuelos were outstretched as they had been at the start as everyone massed together. The watch on her wrist started vibrating, alerting her that it was time. The bells rang, confirming to her and everyone else in Pamplona that Fiesta had ended. Everyone began singing "Pobre de Mí." Poor me. Fiesta is over. Carefully she untied the pañuelo from around her neck, then tied it next to the red Western-patterned one that hadn't moved from her wrist for the past five days.

Stories were told of the highs and lows experienced this year, discussions had about the lives to which people would return, plans for their futures shared—all in a mix of languages. Couples new and old held each other and exchanged "I love yous" as if their first time or their last. Friends and families remarked on wonderful times.

It was the same story as always, told by a new generation. The years, they went by, but the heart of the fiesta, the characters that came and went, always managed to find their way back to this place in some way or fashion.

She pushed through the crowds of runners coming down from their highs and moved down to the streets below, toward where the bulls used to be, used to run. She came to the place where Saint Fermin had been in the wall, gone from his lofty perch. Now people left mementos and candles in his place. Below the Saint's spot a woman sang "Danny Boy." Grace listened for a few moments, struck by the emotion in the lines, *"The summer's gone, and all the roses falling, it's you, it's you must go and I must bide."* Looking down at her unlit candle, eyes blurry with tears, she walked down an alleyway away from the run route and the bull paddock.

She soon came across the group of Americans who had been accompanying Michael. They were arguing, lobbing accusations at each other as they had been for the past five days. She heard the tall, heavily tattooed runner say, "I told him this would happen. No way is this my fault." The more strident soldierly one responded, "No one's blaming you, we all knew the risks." The other three stood by, not knowing what to do. She wanted to go to them, tell them all would be okay, that everything would be alright, but knew it wasn't her place to do so.

A short walk later she came to the church, where people added pañuelos to the doors already turned red with neckerchiefs. Taking the ones tied around her wrist, she carefully knotted them on one of the steel grates on a window, interlacing the red cloths together. Then, in a whisper, she recited lines from Ecclesiastes that she said at the end of every fiesta: *"The sun rises, the sun sets, and then it hurries back to where it rises again."* On her right, candles cast light on a low wall.

Taking the candle she carried, she carefully lit it using one already melting away. Setting it next to the others and bringing her hands together, she offered a prayer, tears returning to her eyes. Poor me, the fiesta is over. The laughter, the tears, the friends new and old, the excess. Michael. All packed into such a short time that had seemed would never end.

Grace watched as the wax dripped down the side of the candle she'd lit. A new song came out of the darkness. "Ya Falta Menos." *Already missing less.* As she watched the candle wax drip down like her own tears, sadness turned to hope. There was always next year, always another fiesta, where things that could have happened would have a chance to come again.

Looking up at the night sky, seeing the constellations illuminated on a moonless night despite the light pollution around her, she wiped her tears and then smiled at the candle. She held that spot for a few more breaths, then started walking, over her shoulder a sign pointing the way to Hospitalario de Pamplona.

# AUTHORS NOTES AND ACKNOWLEDGMENTS

The idea for this book came to me after witnessing my first bullfight. I ran that morning, then found myself in a nosebleed seat that afternoon. After nearly a decade in the Army, it was the first time I'd felt a true, empathetic response to the world around me after my deployments to Afghanistan. Reflecting on that moment, I felt there was a connection between the life cycle of a fighting bull and that of a soldier. This book is my attempt to explore that comparison as I saw it. When you've carried an idea for a book for over ten years, you can't help but think of all the people who entered your life and made it possible.

The first person I need to thank is Dennis Clancy who brought me to Pamplona and taught me how to run. If you are traveling to Pamplona and thinking about running with the bulls, I encourage you to look him up. You won't find a better guide to the streets and how to get through the run in one piece. You also won't find another American who's as daring when it comes to the run. The next person is Alexander Fiske-Harrison, who taught me everything I could want to know and more about what actually happens inside the arena. His blog and his book *Into The Arena: The World Of The Spanish Bullfight* were invaluable in creating this book. Through him I've also had the pleasure of meeting a few Matadors, namely Eduardo Davila Muira who was my inspiration for the prologue. Over the decade I've known him he's given me countless lectures into the Taurine world and I'm looking forward to the next decade where he lectures me on wolves. I also owe an acknowledgment to Juan Jose Padilla, who was the first Matador I got to see in the arena and whom I modeled the matador in this book after, which I don't believe I embellished at all, in fact I might have downplayed him as a character.

Pamplona attracts people who travel there every year to participate and I'm sure I'll miss a bunch of names that I shared the experiences with and deserve recognition; to name a few- Deirdre Carney for sharing stories about her father Matt Carney (the first American runner) and her god father Noelle Chandler both men who've left a lasting legacy on Pamplona. Chloe Phillips for being the life of the party year after year. The Kellerman family who've always been gracious to me. All the runners: Larry Belcher, Jim Hollander, Joe Distler, Angus Macswan, John Hemingway, The Hoskins crew, Jordan Tipples, Angus Ritche, Jeremiah Carroll, Rick Musica, Stephen Ibarra, Leroy Hatfield, Ryan Bennet, Bill Hillman, Jerry Roach, Tom Gowen, Joe Furey, Matthew Clayfield. Anyone who's shared a table and drink with me, as I'm sure there are dozens more names I could add to this list. Most importantly I'd like to thank all the people of Pamplona and the Basque runners who started this tradition and allow us foreigners to come and participate.

The biggest struggle I've had is dealing with life after the Military. I'd like to thank all the friends and family who've helped me along the with that transition. Starting with my sister Megan who's been a constant support for me to lean on. My mother Donna who gave me the ultimate gift by teaching me how to read and her husband Frank. My father, his wife Michelle and her family. My brother Justin. My other brother Andrew and his future wife Stephanie, along with the entire Silva family who's just accepted that we're related at this point. My aunts and uncles, especially my Uncle David who's been my editor from the start and has really been the one to see me get this book finished. My Editor Samantha Zaboski for keeping this manuscript tight and to the point. My Uncles 1SG(RET) John(RIP) and Msgt(RET) Bill Quinn. The Schaffer Family, the Ressler family, the Middleton Clan, the Elrods and the Giacalones-especially Curtis and his wife for constantly housing me when I need it. The Moralez family, especially Maggie for all she's done for the Veterans at SJSU. Dr Elena Klaw, Lindsay Hogden, and Alissa Shaw also at SJSU. My editors Robert Airoldi and Michael Moore for encouraging me to write and for printing it. Ariana Schwartz for being an initial reader. Albert Marquez my Spanish teacher who showed me Spain outside the bullring. My Rugby club the San Jose Seahawks. Dr. Monte Lindmeir and his family. Dr. Shannon Jones and her family in Alberta, Canada. Dr. Michael Hanifen and Dr. Stacey Lowe who, while I was in Interning in Alaska gave me the go ahead to go back to Spain to get a run in. Everyone at Operation Freedom Paws (OFP) Especially Dyan Adinamas for all the help she's given me and the clients at OFP. OFP's Mary Cortani, who I co-authored the book *Four Paws, Two Feet, One Team*, which I believe is my finest literary work, and for Parker-my constant shadow and confidant.

Ultimately this book is dedicated to the GWOT Generation. So, thank you to all of you who served with me in that era, there's a lot of names I'm sure I'll forget and a lot of ranks I'm sure I'll get wrong. Special thanks to 1SG (RET) Casey Coombes and his wife Samantha. CSM Christopher Carey, CSM Thomas Kunnman, COL Nathan Drake, COL John Ford, 1SG (RET) Ricky Elza, 1SG(RET) Vernon Story, 1SG Mike Potter, SFC Terry "Dark Signal" Lawson, SFC(RET) Richard Gatewood, Bobby Struck, SFC(RET) Robert

Savoldy, Ian Lee-Feullit. The three amigos: 1SG Cameron Snider, SFC Sean O'Hara, and SFC Mark Moors All my medics in Voodoo Platoon:, Robert Ward, 1SG Nathan Rose, Michael Bowman (RIP), Paul Espinosa, Ryan Gallagher, Brandon Dussia, Stan Omar, Rusty Mauney, Edgar Patino, Jose Davila, Evan Goff, Chad Hagans, Corey Peters, Joe Carney, COL (RET) Stephen Spencer, Dan Maclaughlin. The organizations that helped shape me: HHT, A Co., B Co and Charlie Rock 1-32 Cavalry Regiment, 1st Brigade combat team, the 101st Airborne and the entire U.S. Army. Jaweed Kharimi and all the interpreters who served the U.S. Army in Afghanistan. My friends in Germany who helped make me a better medic and Soldier: 1SG Jens Pietrzyk, Quentin and Alina Kruse, Margo Clark. James Parker my original climbing partner. Dr. Ryan Drizen and Dr. Roy Ybarra, who helped pick me off the floor when I was at my lowest. Ben Sandoval and Jake Schultz for giving me feedback on this book. Jonathon Pilgram (RIP) and lastly Jedidiah Zillmer (RIP) and all those Veterans who lost the war at home.